Hugo's Voice

and

Other Fictions, Fables

and

Fantasies of Love

Hugo's Voice

and

Other Fictions, Fables and Fantasies of Love

Melvyn Chase

SANTA FE

Sunstone books may be purchased for educational, business, or sales promotional use. For information please write: Special Markets Department, Sunstone Press, P.O. Box 2321, Santa Fe, New Mexico 87504-2321.

Book and cover design › Vicki Ahl
Body typeface › Times New Roman
Printed on acid-free paper

eBook 978-1-61139-556-3

Library of Congress Cataloging-in-Publication Data

Names: Chase, Melvyn, 1938- author.
Title: Hugo's voice : and other fictions, fables and fantasies of love / by Melvyn Chase.
Description: Santa Fe : Sunstone Press, 2018.
Identifiers: LCCN 2018016743 (print) | LCCN 2018022581 (ebook) | ISBN 9781611395563 | ISBN 9781632932303 (softcover : alk. paper)
Subjects: | GSAFD: Love stories.
Classification: LCC PS3603.H3794 (ebook) | LCC PS3603.H3794 A6 2018 (print) | DDC 813/.6--dc23
LC record available at https://lccn.loc.gov/2018016743

WWW.SUNSTONEPRESS.COM
SUNSTONE PRESS / POST OFFICE BOX 2321 / SANTA FE, NM 87504-2321 /USA
(505) 988-4418 / ORDERS ONLY (800) 243-5644 / FAX (505) 988-1025

ISBN 978-1-63293-563-2

To storytellers,
mythmakers and fabulists everywhere,
who engage our imaginations and enrich our lives.

Contents

Prologue: Storytellers

My father wasn't a writer, but he really knew how to tell a story, how to make it come to life. In fact, I'm from a *family* of storytellers. We would sit around the kitchen table at dinner or afterwards and tell stories—my father and mother, my grandparents (my mother's parents who lived with us), my sister (who was eight years older than me). When I was very young, I just listened, learning how to paint people and places and feelings with words. Finally, when I was ready, when I was brave enough, I chimed in with my own stories.

I lived with my parents until I was twenty, in an apartment house on Foster Avenue in Brooklyn. It was a Jewish neighborhood, with a sizable sprinkling of Italians and Irish. Most of the Jews lived in apartment houses, unless the father was a doctor or lawyer. The *goyim*, the Gentiles, even the ones who weren't rich, usually owned their own homes. "Private houses," we called them, as if privacy was a luxury we couldn't afford.

One luxury my family *could* afford was storytelling.

Some of the stories were links to the past. For the children, it was all we knew about our roots. All four of my grandparents were immigrants, who came to this country from the Ukraine around the turn of the twentieth century. Their stories were memories of the Old Country, awful memories.

My mother's father told about how *his* father, the village blacksmith, was killed by a Cossack.

"Mit zayn shverd—hat im geharget!"

"Killed him with his sword," my father whispered.

And no matter how many times my grandfather told that story, it always brought tears to his eyes. He could still be that little boy more than seventy years ago, witnessing that horrific scene.

My other grandparents, my father's parents, died when I was very young. I don't remember them, except from photographs and a few soundless, voiceless home movies that my father took—everyone walking quickly, stiffly, waving at the camera and laughing self-consciously.

One day—I must have been about fourteen—my father told me a very surprising story:

"In the Old Country, Grandpa was married and had two young children, a son and a daughter. And when he told his wife they were going to America, she said, 'Not me. This is my home and I don't want to leave.' They argued about this for days. Neither of them backed down. Finally Grandpa said, 'I'm going and I'll take Max' (their son) 'and you can stay here with Rosie' (their daughter). And that's what they did."

"So they got a divorce and Grandpa came here?" I asked.

"*Maybe* they got a divorce. I doubt it. When Grandpa came here, he met your Grandmother and married her. And God bless her, she always loved Max as much as she loved me."

I had mixed feelings about this revelation. But to a fourteen-year-old, it was kind of exciting to discover that one of his grandfathers was a bigamist!

When my son and daughter were in their twenties—and not before—I confessed that my best friend Dave and I hitchhiked to St. Louis one summer and to New Orleans the next.

"We were juniors in college. We told our parents a friend was driving us."

"You lied!" my daughter said, shaking her finger at me.

"We reached St. Louis in six days," I said, ignoring the reprimand. "We got rides from salesmen, soldiers, people who just wanted to talk to somebody. We were two skinny kids who didn't look dangerous."

"But you never know what kind of weirdos may pick you up," my son said. "Isn't that what you always told us?"

"It's much riskier nowadays," I offered lamely.

"So you didn't meet any weirdos?"

"A few, yes," I admitted. "Crazy drivers, maybe. Life-threatening, no."

They stared at me intensely, disapprovingly, comically.

"The next summer, we hitched down to New Orleans," I said, adding quickly in a stage whisper, "and spent a night in jail in Mississippi."

"My God!" my daughter wailed, in mock outrage.

"So you're wanted in three states?" my son said.

I corrected him. "It's only *two* states."

My confession freed my son and daughter to gleefully (and with conspiratorial looks) give as good as they got, telling me eyebrow-raising stories about their own teen-age years—stories that began "You never knew about the time..."

No doubt about it: in my family, the story-telling tradition lives on.

But it's really a universal tradition.

We tell stories in so many ways and so many places. At the dinner table, around the campfire, in books, on stage, in movies, on television. And reaching further back in time, in the fables, myths and legends we share.

Storytelling is usually a blend of fact and fiction. There is a clandestine core of reality in our myths—and a lesson, perhaps, or a warning. And our truths are often touched by fantasy.

History sadly shows that our animal instincts and urges too often overpower the better angels of our nature. But there is more to us than instincts and urges. There is in us a deep-seated need to share memories and fantasies and feelings, the joy of love and the pain of loneliness. Storytelling is one way we share, one way we affirm our humanity.

Here are some stories I'd like to share with you.

Why I Never Got Married

"Why didn't you ever get married?"

Angela, my twenty-five-year-old niece, has often asked me that question and I have responded with the customary cliches: "I just never found the right girl. I didn't think I could ever settle down. I guess I'm too set in my ways."

She's a San Francisco journalist with a surprisingly influential political blog. I live a continent away in New York City, so we rarely see each other. Except at her mother's (my sister Donna's) annual birthday bash at Donna's home on Long Island. My brother-in-law invents a "theme" for each party, writes a dreadful poem ("She's thirty/but still flirty"), assembles an intentionally embarrassing video and emcees a comedy skit usually starring himself and his three children. It's an event that generates much heat and light and laughter. My only assignment is to play the role of a grouchy spectator—that is, to play myself.

"Why didn't you ever get married?"

It was a comfortable, breezy September evening. The party was winding down. Both of Angela's brothers were in the den with their father, watching a Yankee game. Their wives were chatting with the Birthday Girl as they helped her clear away the dishes and debris. Their assorted children were eating or playing soccer in the back yard. Angela and I were drinking wine out on the deck.

"I could ask you the same question," I said.

She shook her head impatiently. "I'm too young, too focused on my career. And sex is everywhere. Why tie myself down?"

She smiled and added, "What's your excuse?"

"Do I need an excuse?"

"You can't answer a question with a question. Only Jewish people are allowed to do that."

"Ha!" I laughed.

"Even now, old as you are, you're in pretty good shape," she said.

"Fifty-eight is *not* old."

Ignoring my faux outrage, she said, "You're not bad looking, you know. And you're reasonably intelligent. Very successful, too."

She sighed, "And so terribly alone."

"Alone is not necessarily terrible."

She sipped her wine, studying me with her merciless blue eyes.

"If I had only met someone like you," I suggested.

"Don't give me that crap," she said.

"Maybe you're asking a question that's too personal."

Her eyes softened. Her voice did, too.

"I'm used to asking personal questions," Angela explained. "That's my job."

"I know. And you're damn good at it."

She looked up at the darkening sky, watched the first stars begin to appear.

"I wonder what they think of us," she said.

"The stars? They don't think. They just turn hydrogen into helium."

Angela groaned. "How romantic!"

We sat quietly for a few minutes, refilled our glasses and enjoyed the light-bodied Pinot Noir. The wine, the warm breeze, the sounds of the children playing, the emerging stars—it was all so peaceful.

"All right, Angela," I said. "I'll tell you why I never got married."

She looked skeptical.

"I'm not joking," I said. "I'll tell you why, but you might not believe me."

"I reserve the right to ask follow-up questions. That's the sign of a good interviewer."

I nodded my approval. She leaned forward and waited.

"I guess I was about your age," I began, "fresh out of law school. I was hired by Miller Crain, not a white-shoe firm but close enough. And I lucked out on my first assignment: doing the grunt work for Thad Crocker on a big patent infringement case."

"Never heard of him."

"He was one of those celebrity lawyers. He knew how to promote himself. Keep his name in the headlines."

"With patent infringement?" Angela wondered. "Not exactly a hot topic."

"He *made* it a hot topic," I said. "He turned an allegedly stolen software system into a sin against humanity."

"And you were along for the ride."

"Yes. Just a bag man. But I learned a lot."

She nodded and said, "And that's why you never got married?"

"Be patient. I'm getting there."

"Patience is not my thing."

"Crocker won," I said. "And he owed me: I had found a letter that clinched the case."

"He gave you credit for it?"

"Of course not. But he had me assigned—full time—to him."

Angela sipped her wine and said, "So you fell in love with him, and that's why you never got married?"

Naturally, I didn't dignify that comment with a response.

Instead, I went on, "One of his clients was an opera star. The soprano, Florence Perry."

Angela nodded. "I have a couple of her CDs. She was amazing. She had a long, brilliant career."

"Almost 50 years, and her voice never seemed to age."

"She died a couple of years ago," Angela remembered. "I think she was in her nineties."

"Florence Perry was in a contract dispute with the Met. Thad Crocker was handling it. He asked me to find out if there were any verbal agreements the Met made with her before they signed her contract."

"Wouldn't a written contract matter more?" Angela asked.

"Yes, but if he could create doubt....That was what he was after. Was the Met playing fair?"

"So you met Florence Perry."

"I did. She and her husband lived in one of those huge apartments in a turn-of-the-century building on West End Avenue in Manhattan. High ceilings. Enormous rooms."

"What was she like?" Angela asked.

"Gracious. Beautiful. Reserved. She had been a leading soprano for more than twenty-five years, but she seemed so young. If I didn't know who she was, I would have guessed she was thirty or thirty-five. But she must have been almost fifty."

"She was very lucky."

I hesitated for a long moment, then said, "I also met her husband.

James Perry. I was not impressed. He was a rather dull man, not particularly attractive. And he *looked* much older than her."

"You mean he *was* much older."

I didn't correct myself.

"As the case progressed," I said, "I got to know the Perrys. I ended up spending a lot of time with James—waiting for Florence to spare me a few minutes of *her* time. And the better I knew him, the harder it was to understand why Florence didn't leave him. Why was she faithful to this cipher?"

"True love?" Angela said.

"True love," I agreed. "One afternoon, when I was waiting for Florence to return from a rehearsal, James and I shared a bottle of wine. The way we're doing now. And he began to talk about Florence. How much he loved her. How he didn't deserve someone so wonderful, so beautiful, so talented. And then he said, 'If I wanted to keep her, I knew I would have to give her something special—a gift that no one else would give her. And that's what I did.'"

Angela, still expecting a punchline, waited for me to continue.

"James was the same age as Florence," I said. "He knew that what mattered most to her was keeping her voice, her talent, for as long as she could. So he gave her the one priceless thing he could offer: his youth. Twenty more years for her to be young. Twenty years of youth added to her life and subtracted from his."

Angela frowned.

"You're not serious," she said.

"I didn't think you would believe me."

"Of course I don't. It's impossible."

"I won't argue with you, Angela," I said, with a quizzical smile.

I drank some wine, glanced at the stars for a moment and gave her the answer she was waiting for.

"You asked me why I never got married. How could I possibly love someone the way James loved Florence? How could I give any woman the kind of gift he gave her? I'm too selfish to do that. I guess I don't really have it in me to love anyone that way."

Angela leaned back and sighed.

"And that's why I never got married."

Hugo's Voice

Silence is all we dread.
There's Ransom in a Voice—
But Silence is Infinity.
—Emily Dickinson

I

Hugo Strauss was a quiet man. He could rarely find the right words. For the past fifteen years, he had worked in the Fairfield-Connecticut jewelry store owned by his uncle, Myron Shaw, his mother's brother. Hugo repaired injured necklaces, brooches, rings. A tall, slender man, he bent double over the jeweler's bench in a room at the back of the shop, the ventilator humming its relentless monotone as it filtered the air. A dust mask, like a highwayman's bandana, covered Hugo's nose and mouth as he studied his wounded patients through thick magnifying lenses, his long fingers gracefully manipulating tiny pliers and drills, guiding the fierce, healing flame of a soldering torch, or restoring a gold or silver sheen with a few rapid strokes of a polisher's wheel.

At busy times, Hugo could even fill in as a salesman. The buyer-seller dialogue was a familiar ritual—predictable variations on a theme, like the riffs of a blues guitar. So he was comfortable praising the sinister play of colors in an opal, the pristine clarity of a diamond, the delicate, lacy latticework of a pendant.

When he tried to propose to Caroline, he hesitated. Stammered.

She squeezed his hand. Her fingers gripped his tightly, masterfully, as she said, "Yes, I'll marry you."

In the eight years of their marriage, Caroline often finished his sentences with the final word on their decisions.

A few days after her third miscarriage, clouds shadowed her blue eyes. She watched him suspiciously, as if she thought he was trying to deceive her.

She began to drink a glass of wine, sometimes two, every night before dinner. And mirroring Hugo, she rarely spoke.

Caroline needed to be in control. That was probably why she married Hugo. She had planned her pregnancies. When those plans didn't work out, again and again, he was saddened but she was angry. She had done her best, hadn't she? And she had failed. She had lost control.

He waited (silently) for her to break the silence.

One evening, her wine glass refilled, she said, "Not again."

She seemed disappointed that he didn't react. She sipped her wine.

Hugo echoed, "Not again."

"Do you understand me?"

"Yes."

Her voice was soft and harsh, like the whisper of a cruel rumor: "I don't need a child."

That was her new plan.

He could have said, "Maybe *we* need a child. We could adopt."

But he could feel the heat of her anger. Her outrage. He said nothing but she knew he was angry, too.

Would we be able to love a child? he wondered. *Nurture it. Make it better than us. Could a child make* us *better, too?*

But every day after that, fragments of her anger, his disappointment, fluttered between them like sullen, invisible curtains.

It wasn't the only barrier that separated them. Intimacy had never been easy. They shared occasional moments of ease, of pleasure, but kept their longings and their pain to themselves. Sexual intimacy was especially difficult. Their passion was intense but sporadic. Spasms in the dark. Now it became silent, without a pretense of tenderness. A venting of desire, intentionally infertile.

He still fantasized about sex, sometimes remembering a summer at his parents' cabin at Candlewood Lake. He was sixteen. Stereotypically awkward. Not dating yet. She was lean and athletic, nearly two years older. She didn't sympathize with his shyness, but was amused by it. She fed his hunger, stoked it. She tutored him. After two weeks, she lost interest in him and found pleasure elsewhere. It wasn't her face or body he remembered. Or even her heat. It was her freedom.

After that there were other women. Nothing long-term. He met Caroline when he was twenty-two and she was nineteen. And then there were no others.

He wondered if Caroline had her own fantasies.

Everyone has fantasies, don't they?

He never had the courage to ask her, afraid if she did have them. Afraid if she didn't.

In the eighth year of their marriage, at breakfast on a raw Fall morning, Caroline was looking out the kitchen window at a surly sky.

She said, "You know..."

When she was about to fill in the blanks, her heart suddenly stopped beating.

Hugo was left without his voice.

II

Aunt Esther, Uncle Myron's wife, often invited Hugo for dinner, usually on a Thursday night. She was a good cook. Her specialties: a hearty chicken-livers-and-rice concoction, and a thick beef stew packed with vegetables and potatoes. Much tastier than the bland Spartan meals he prepared for himself. Esther had taught Caroline how to make both dishes, but his wife had never mastered them. Something was missing.

"Geoffrey called last night," Esther said as she ladled out the portions of stew.

"How is he?" Hugo asked.

"He won't talk to *me*," Myron complained, shaking his head.

"You don't *talk*, you *argue*," Esther said softly, as if whispering dulled the cutting edge of her words.

Myron sighed and gestured dismissively with his hand.

"I don't know what the hell he wants from me," he said.

"To listen to him, maybe."

Esther turned to Hugo and said, "They're so far away."

"Seattle," Myron said, as if he were saying "Hell."

Geoffrey was an Assistant Professor of Art History at the University of Washington.

Hugo nodded.

"Why not Mars?" Myron asked.

"They both have good jobs," Esther said.

"It rains all the time out there," Myron muttered.

"Give him a call." she said. "Just don't talk politics."

"He's practically a communist," Myron said.

"He's not!" Esther disagreed. "He's a whatayacallit—a socialist."

Myron snorted, "Communists. Socialists. It's the same thing."

Esther answered him with a narrow-eyed look.

They ate in silence for a few minutes.

Then, in her motherly voice, Esther broke the silence.

"Are you seeing anyone, Hugo?"

Hugo shook his head.

"You're still a young man," she said. "Caroline's been gone a long time. Three years already."

"You got to move on," Myron added.

Hugo shrugged. "I go out."

Esther gently prodded. "But there's nobody special?"

"Nobody."

"It's the same thing with Vivian," Myron said.

"She has very high standards," Esther parried.

Myron laughed. "High standards? So why did she marry that *shlemiel*?"

Vivian, their thirty-five-year-old daughter, got married when she was twenty and divorced before she was twenty-two.

"She was a kid," Esther said. "She didn't know what she was doing."

"If she waits much longer, she'll be too old to have children. It may be too late already."

Esther nodded agreement. "It's a different world now. I don't think that matters to her." She turned to Hugo. "She makes a very good living." (She was a CPA.) "She has a beautiful apartment in Chelsea. Two bathrooms." ("One and a half," Myron interjected.) "A terrace. She goes to Europe or the Caribbean every year and she has plenty of men in her life. She's doing fine."

Myron shrugged and asked for another portion of stew.

"Hugo," he said, "you don't want to hear this again, but..."

"If he doesn't want to hear it," Esther said, "don't say it."

"Hugo, it's a waste," Myron said. "You're wasting your talent. You should be *making* jewelry. *Creating* it, not just fixing it."

"I don't know..."

"Berger still asks me about you."

Joe Berger owned the Manhattan company that manufactured the pieces designed by Hugo's mother and, later, Hugo's designs.

"When you first came to work for me..."

"I haven't done it in a long time."

"Your mother taught you everything she knew," Myron said. "And she was the best in the business."

Hugo remembered what his mother once said to him: "You learned the craft, but not the art."

Hugo shook his head.

"I'm gonna be a pest," Myron said. "I'm gonna keep after you."

"Leave him alone," Esther said.

Hugo quietly ate his stew.

III

On Sunday afternoons during the National Football League season, Hugo watched games at a sports bar, K-J's, on Route 25 in Monroe. Sometimes he also went there for the Sunday- or Monday-night games.

He didn't meet people from Fairfield there. He wore a *Tom Brady/ Boston Patriots* sweatshirt. He drank beer. He groaned or cheered or howled when others did. He could be a member of the club without being anyone's friend.

The owners of the bar, Kenny and Jack (K and J), called him "Yoog" for short. (Everyone did.) Poured his Corona beer. Kept the peanut and pretzel bowls filled.

A beefy sixty-year-old Irishman, Kevin Kelly, enjoyed *Yoog's* company because Kevin never stopped talking and Hugo never interrupted him.

"That look in Brady's eyes," Kevin might say. "The eye of the fuckin' tiger."

Hugo would nod.

"The best in the business."

"The best."

"Ever!"

"Ever."

"Damn straight," Kevin would say and continue with a stream-of-consciousness that Hugo could acknowledge silently or with an occasional word or two.

That was more than enough for Kevin, who never talked to Hugo about anything other than football.

On those Sundays and Mondays, Hugo spent a few comfortable hours. He enjoyed the beer. And the football games offered him a guilty pleasure: a painless taste of violence.

One Sunday afternoon, Kevin arrived a little late. He had company. A plump, thirtyish red-headed woman wearing a Patriots sweatshirt and a pair of jeans one size too small.

"Yoog—Hugo, this is my daughter Margaret," Kevin said.

"Nice to meet you," Margaret said. "My dad tells me you're great pals."

"We are."

She smiled, shook his hand and said, "Maybe we can be friends, too, huh?"

"Sure."

Margaret held his hand for another long, uncomfortable moment and kept smiling. Then she sat down at the bar between Hugo and Kevin.

She didn't pay any attention to the game.

"You're in the jewelry business?" she asked.

"Yes."

"Whatta pass!" Kevin said. "That goddamn Brady's a genius."

"That's a good business, I bet," she said.

"Yes."

"You own the store?"

"My uncle does."

"He gets rid of the ball so fuckin' fast!" Kevin said, then whispered, "Sorry, honey."

"Don't worry about it," Margaret said. "I heard the word before," and she laughed.

Hugo thought that her teeth were too big for her mouth, as if she had borrowed the teeth of a carnivore.

He was getting angry. He wanted to watch the game and listen to Kevin.

"I love jewelry," she said, reaching up to touch one of her huge silver earrings.

"Women do."

"Maybe I should get to know you better," she said and laughed again.

Hugo nodded.

"He dropped the goddamn ball," Kevin groaned and slapped the bar.

"Good pass, too," Hugo said.

Margaret was a wall between him and Kevin, an aggressive, fidgety wall. The whole afternoon.

She went to the Ladies Room at half-time.

Kevin put his heavy hand on Hugo's shoulder.

"I'm sorry I brought her," Kevin said. "I was talkin' about you the other day. She's divorced—not in the eyes of the Church, of course. Has two kids. She's huntin' around for a husband."

He looked deep into Hugo's eyes and said, "Listen, Yoog. You don't have to call her. Or see her. Really, believe me. Makes no difference to me."

Late in the third quarter, Margaret gave him her phone number. He didn't call her. And Kevin never mentioned her again.

IV

After Caroline died, Hugo continued to live in their house. Actually, it was *his* house: his parents had left it to him. It was on an acre of land near Fairfield University, in a pleasant, tree-shaded neighborhood.

He turned one of the bedrooms, which was supposed to become the nursery, into a guest room, although he never invited any guests. Except when a woman stayed the night, which happened occasionally: Hugo always slept with her in the guest room.

He ate in the kitchen and left the dining room untouched. A cleaning woman came every two weeks to tidy up but she had very little to do.

At the back of the house was a studio with a wall of broad picture windows and skylights in a high, slanted ceiling. The studio was furnished with an easel, a work table, a bookshelf packed with art books, and a cabinet filled with oil paints, charcoal, pastels and drawing pads. A CD player with two Bose speakers sat on one corner of the work table.

The wall opposite the windows was crowded with paintings—half a dozen vibrant, violent pieces by his father, several minutely detailed jewelry designs by his mother, and four of Hugo's highly stylized Boston street scenes, completed more than five years ago. He had painted nothing since then.

He often sat in the studio reading, listening to Bruckner, Mozart and classic jazz, sketching, or enjoying the view of his English garden, which he maintained in carefully arranged disarray—splashes of shapes and colors in chaotic splendor.

"It's my way of painting now," he told his friend, Jamie Meyers.

In warm weather, he would find a shaded spot in the garden, drink a chilled white wine and immerse himself in what he called his "private Eden."

It was a cloudy, starless November night a week after Hugo's grim

Sunday with Margaret. He was in the studio enjoying a slab of chocolate layer cake and a cup of coffee, when Jamie called.

He and Jamie had been close friends since elementary school.

"What's cooking, Hugo?"

"See the Pats Sunday?"

"I couldn't," Jamie said. "Sunday is *family* day."

Hugo laughed. "Caroline always let me watch."

"I used to tell Louise that. I told her, 'Caroline's a ballbuster and she lets Hugo watch football.' Didn't help."

"Sorry."

"It'd be good for my boys, too," Jamie said.

"How's things at work?"

"Garrison's a real prick," Jamie moaned. "Two minutes after he's promoted, he's king of the world. He's too *important* to have lunch with me."

"Mmmm."

"He's got an office with a *door* now."

"A door."

"And a goddamn plant."

"A plant."

"And now he hangs out with the boss all the time."

"Bastard."

After a pause, Jamie asked, "You busy Saturday night?"

Hugo knew what was coming.

"No."

"Louise has this friend at work..."

"Divorced," Hugo said. "Desperate."

Jamie laughed. "You get the picture."

Hugo sighed.

"You free?" Jamie asked.

"Sure."

"She lives in Trumbull. I don't have her address handy. I'll call you back with it."

"Can't wait."

"Meet us at The Watermill at seven-thirty. We'll go to a movie afterward."

"Okay."

"You never know..." Jamie said.

"Yeah, sure."

Hugo's date, Laura, was a soft-spoken, pleasant young woman. Rather tall. Rather pretty. But not so good at making conversation with a man who was no help.

On the way to the restaurant, Laura asked, "You're a jeweler?"

"Yes."

"Louise said you *fix* jewelry, right?"

"Right."

"You're not a salesman?"

"Right."

"Where's your store?"

"Fairfield."

Laura waited for more information. Silence.

"Did you go to school for that?" she asked.

"No."

Silence.

"You just picked it up?"

"My mother taught me."

"So it's like a family business."

Hugo nodded.

Laura searched for another question.

"You ever *make* jewelry?" she asked. "Like design it, I mean."

"Just fix it."

Hugo knew she was struggling, but he wouldn't let himself feel sorry for her or try to encourage her.

He was never interested in nice women who needed someone to love. He didn't know why. Sometimes he wasn't even sure that he had loved Caroline.

Why don't I miss her? I hardly even remember her.

It was as if their marriage were a movie he had seen years ago. A black-and-white movie.

He remembered the girl at Candlewood Lake. He wanted to remember her. He had met other women like her, who didn't ask him for anything more than pleasure. Who didn't demand anything more. Not love. Not sharing. Not "forever." Who smiled when they said Goodbye. Those are the women he wanted to meet.

Louise did most of the talking at dinner, explaining Hugo to Laura and Laura to Hugo.

"Hugo's a real artist," Louise said. "Went to art school and everything."

"Long ago," Hugo said.

"His mother and father were artists, too," Louise continued.

"Both of them?"

"Yes. His mother was famous, wasn't she?"

"Kind of," Hugo said.

"A famous jewelry designer," Louise added.

"You've got to be lucky. To have talent," Laura said.

"Well *you've* got talent," Louise insisted. "For numbers, right?"

Laura smiled in agreement.

Louise turned to Hugo.

"Laura's getting her Master's at night. In accounting."

"Your cousin Vivian's a CPA, isn't she?" Jamie asked.

"Yes."

"That's a great profession," Louise said. "Big bucks."

"The exam is very hard," Laura observed.

Louise laughed. "Not too hard for *you*, I bet."

"Well..."

"Come on," Louise said. "You'll ace it."

Laura smiled weakly. "We'll see."

Hugo and Laura were both relieved when they left the restaurant for the movie theatre.

The film they saw was a hit romantic comedy. Hugo couldn't understand why. He thought the characters were infantile, the jokes stale and the outcome predictable. The audience roared with laughter. He thought the movie would never end.

When it did, Louise asked, "Anyone for coffee and dessert?"

That suggestion lost 3-1.

On the way back to her apartment, Laura asked, "Did you think the movie was funny?"

"No."

"Me, neither."

Hugo wanted to go home. He was tired.

He looked forward to watching football tomorrow afternoon, drinking Corona beer and agreeing with Kevin Kelly.

Outside her door, Laura said,"Thanks. I had a good time. Want to come in for coffee? Or a drink?"

"No, thanks."

He wished he could have said more, but he couldn't.

He didn't kiss her. He shook her hand.

He watched the door close behind her.

He tried not to feel guilty, but he did.

V

A few mornings later Uncle Myron said, "I have a gift for you."

Myron's tepid smile implied that it was an unwelcome gift.

"I've signed you up for a figure drawing class with Gary Steiner," Myron said. "My treat."

"I don't..."

"He was a friend of your father's."

"Yes."

"A friend of yours, too?"

"No."

"It'll be good for you."

"Not something I need."

"You won't learn anything," Myron said. "You're way past that. But it'll give you a little push. Tune you up. Get you in the mood again."

"For what?"

"You *know* what," Myron said.

"I still do some sketching."

"A little more can't hurt."

"Can't help."

Myron insisted.

Hugo, averse to arguing, finally relented.

Gary Steiner was, in the words of his publicist, a "celebrated fashion illustrator". A handsome, arrogant man, he claimed to know everybody who was anybody, and boasted of the love affairs that proved it.

Hugo remembered him as the imp of perversity. If you said *Yes* he would, on principle, say *No*.

Hugo's father enjoyed Gary. Hugo's mother endured him. Hugo tried to avoid him, keeping silent, even when provoked. Especially when provoked. He hadn't seen Gary in more than ten years, nor had he missed him.

Gary lived with his second wife and two teenage daughters in a gargantuan house in Fairfield's Southport section on the shore of Long Island

Sound. It was a pricey neighborhood which preferred to think of itself as a separate town.

Gary usually had half a dozen students. He didn't need the money, but his classes were expensive anyway: he asserted that his occasional comments—his very presence—were of enormous value and, apparently, his acolytes agreed.

Hugo's first class was on an icy night in early December, which was even colder by the Sound. A fierce, mean-spirited wind whistled across the churning water.

Inside Gary's spacious studio, though, it was warm as fresh-baked bread. On a low platform in the center of the room sat a fortyish woman, the model, in a faux silk robe. She was reading PEOPLE magazine. The platform was surrounded by easels and stools. Near it, a handful of students was gathered around the maestro.

Hugo tentatively joined the group.

"Line. Texture," Gary said, gesturing lightly with his hand, as if he were conducting a silent symphony. "Trust me. Everything else will follow."

Bromides, Hugo thought, *and oh so dramatic.*

There were five other students: two well-dressed, well-groomed, middle-aged (but miraculously wrinkle-free) women, who clearly worshiped Gary. A gaunt young man who appeared to take himself very seriously. A restless young woman who kept frowning as if she wasn't sure why she was there.

And another woman, in a black sweater and black jeans. A patterned scarf, a splash of contrasting colors, was draped around her neck and across her shoulders.

Hugo was certain he had never seen her before but, at the same time, he felt that he *had.* It was as if her image was already stored in his memory, and she had just made it real.

He studied her, unable to understand why she affected him the way she did.

She was in her late twenties or early thirties. She stood very still, her hands on her hips, watching Gary but not reacting to what he said.

Guarded. Aloof.

Her eyes were dark. Her nose, slightly arched and fine-boned.

Beautiful? Not quite.

Her mouth, a little too full, too wide.

A hint of passion?

Her straight, dark hair was cut short and prematurely streaked with gray.

Beauty-salon gray?

He was confused.

"Could this be Hugo Strauss?" Gary asked, in a tone lightly tinged with acid.

As the woman in black turned toward him, Hugo turned toward Gary. But the image of the woman's face lingered.

"It *is*," Hugo said, anticipating a minute or two of embarrassment.

Gary addressed the class: "Hugo's mother and father were very talented artists. Dear friends of mine. Both deceased, alas."

Gary paused, eyes downcast, the mask of tragedy. Then he looked up at Hugo and said, "I seem to remember that you had abandoned the Arts. Has the Prodigal Son returned?"

"Maybe."

Gary nodded. "Well, perhaps we can win one for the Arts."

He smiled and shrugged, implying that the game was already lost, and said, "Let us begin."

The model removed her robe and, following Gary's instructions, settled into her first pose. Hugo propped up his pad on an easel and prepared to draw.

He focused on the model, the shape of her torso, the light and shadows. He sketched a few tentative lines, stopped. He tried to relax.

He wasn't uneasy because of Gary. It was because of the woman in black.

She was two easels away, her expression still fixed, seemingly indifferent. And yet her hands and eyes were busily at work.

I'm being absurd, he thought. *She's just another woman.*

But he was fascinated by her. She was an odd alloy of youth and maturity. Her skin was stretched tautly over the bones of her face. She moved with athletic grace. But her hair was already turning gray in stark streaks that, he decided, were too amorphous to be artificial.

She didn't seem to notice anyone around her, not even Gary. She was under control, keeping herself, her feelings, to herself. Only her eyes and hands belonged to the class, to the moment.

Hugo forced himself to examine the model so he could translate the curves of her body into lines on paper.

He was rusty but as he worked, his muscle memory began to revive the easy rhythm of quick, definitive strokes; the instantaneous link between eye and hand.

Gary was cruising around the easels, whispering suggestions. He leaned over the shoulder of the woman in black, too closely. He said something to her. She nodded, said a word or two and continued to draw. Gary kept watching her, then moved on.

When he reached Hugo, he said nothing.

Hugo concentrated on the shape of the model's hip, plotted the line in his mind's eye before he drew it, and followed that imaginary stroke.

Gary said two words, *sotto voce*: "Well done". And then moved on.

For the rest of the night—almost two hours—Hugo kept reaching into his past, reawakening his skills.

Every now and again, he would look over at the woman in black. She never looked at him.

He took a break after an hour or so and managed to catch a glimpse of her work. From what he could see, she was talented but still raw. Unschooled.

When they left Gary's studio, he tried to catch up with her to say Goodnight but she was too quick for him.

VI

That Friday night, the jewelry store stayed open until ten. Christmas and Hanukkah were imminent and Myron's "perfect Holiday gifts for *her*" and "rock-bottom prices for *him*" attracted a crowd of browsers and buyers.

The mark-up on jewelry averaged 300%, so a 30% discount, which sounded substantial, was virtually painless for Myron.

At ten-thirty that night, Hugo and his uncle were drinking fresh-brewed coffee in the locker room behind the store.

"How was the class?" Myron asked.

Until now, they had been too busy to talk about it.

"Fine."

"Did you enjoy it?"

Hugo nodded Yes.

"Did Steiner remember you?"

"He told the class about my Mom and Dad."

"Did you get a *feeling* about what you were doing?"

"I think so."

Myron pressed his fist against his heart and said, "Let yourself go. Get into that *artistic* mood."

"I'll do my best."

"Thanks. That's all I ask."

The phone rang.

It was Jamie.

He must have tried to reach me at home.

"Why're you calling so late?" Hugo wondered.

"It's Barney. He's at my place. In bad shape."

"What's wrong?"

"He and his wife are splitting up," Jamie whispered.

"Why?"

"Long story. Can you come over?"

"Now?"

"Please," Jamie said.

"All right."

Barney Whitman was a high school friend of theirs whom they met occasionally for dinner. He was a lawyer with a modest, small-town practice in Orange, Connecticut. His wife owned a high-end clothing boutique in Greenwich.

When Hugo arrived at Jamie's house, Louise met him at the door. She was not in a welcoming mood.

She cautioned Hugo to speak softly: "The kids are asleep."

She took his coat and hung it on a rack in the hallway. She pointed to the closed door of the den/TV room and went upstairs.

Jamie was sitting in his favorite chair, a director's chair, facing Barney, who was sprawled on the couch.

Ever since they had known him, Barney had sprawled through life. He was big-boned, awkward, never able to sit up straight or avoid bumping into furniture or people. He was also easy-going and sentimental. Not the ideal nature for a lawyer.

Hugo sat down in a leather chair across from Barney.

"What happened?" Hugo asked.

Barney leaned to one side, then the other. His eyes were focused somewhere in space. He started to say something. Stopped. Sighed.

"Marcie...asked me...to leave," he said, softly.

Hugo waited for him to continue, but he didn't. He just kept lurching from side to side.

"She's been fooling around for a while," Jamie said. "She's got a boyfriend."

"Yeah," Barney whispered.

"She want a divorce?" Hugo asked.

"Yeah," Barney said.

"She sent their kid to her mother," Jamie added.

"Yeah," Barney repeated. Lurch, lurch.

"In New Haven," Jamie said.

Barney's face reddened. His mouth puckered. His eyes filled with tears.

"She said...she said she was just a kid...when we got married," he moaned.

"What was she?" Jamie asked. "Nineteen? Twenty?"

"Nineteen."

Jamie nodded. "Yeah. Very young."

Hugo wanted to sympathize with Barney, but he only felt embarrassed for him.

"She said she grew up," Barney said. "Made something of herself. I didn't."

He wiped his eyes with his thick fingers."What'll I do?" he moaned.

Jamie stood up and patted Barney's shoulder.

"I think we could all use a beer," he said.

Barney kept staring into space.

Jamie opened the door carefully, and quietly closed it behind him.

Hugo didn't say anything. Barney kept sniffling and wiping tears away.

His wife knows how to hurt him, Hugo thought. *It's easy for her.*

Barney had always been a victim. A sad story waiting to happen.

It's not so different for Jamie. Everything Louise does is for the kids. Nothing for him.

He thought of Caroline.

There were happy times. Why is it so hard to remember them?

Jamie came back into the room, practically on tip-toes. He handed an open beer bottle to Barney, one to Hugo and kept one for himself.

Would the woman in black be any different? Maybe just a different kind of pain.

That's what Hugo said to himself but he didn't quite believe it.

They drank their beer. Barney stopped crying.

After a few quiet minutes, he said, "I knew she was fooling around. I told her I knew."

"What did she say?" Jamie asked.

"She didn't care."

"You're a lawyer," Jamie said. "You can handle the divorce, right? Make it tough for her."

Barney shook his head. "No. I don't want to make any trouble."

Jamie couldn't believe it. "*She's* the one making trouble, isn't she?"

Barney ignored Jamie's comment.

"I called my sister," he said. "In Long Island. I'm staying with her for a while."

Jamie looked at Hugo and shook his head as if to say, "Do you believe this guy?"

But he said, "That's good. Being with family."

"It's a long drive," Barney said. "Too late to start tonight. Can I crash here, Jamie? Just for tonight?"

Jamie frowned.

Louise would kill him, Hugo thought.

"I've got room," Hugo offered. "A convertible couch in the den."

Jamie smiled a sad smile.

Hugo didn't consider putting Barney in the guest room. If he did, he would never be able to think of the bed in that room without seeing Barney sprawled all over it.

VII

At Hugo's second drawing class, he managed to position himself next to the woman in black.

But tonight she wasn't in black. She was wearing a dark green turtleneck sweater and green slacks a shade lighter. An airy brooch of silver latticework and rainbow-splashed acetate added an accent of color.

At the beginning of the class, Gary greeted each student by name.

Her name is Frances. Does she call herself Fran?

The model was a slender, thirty-something man whose sinuous poses and white, hairless body seemed abstract and almost unreal.

Because Frances was so close to him, Hugo worked more carefully, intensely, hoping that his skill would impress her.

As he worked, he managed to complete his mental portrait of her.

She was tall: only a few inches under six feet.

She probably prefers tall men. Like me.

She was solidly built. Shapely.

A beautiful arc to her body. Strong. Tightly wound.

Her earlobe was pierced twice, but she wasn't wearing earrings.

Her brooch is flashy. Stylish.

Close up, she looked younger. Now he was certain that the gray streaks in her hair were an anomaly, not an affectation.

Her eyes are dark. Sad? Defiant?

"I don't think you need this class."

She had started the conversation. Her voice was husky, without warmth.

Hugo said, "It's a refresher. I've studied art."

"I thought so." She pointed to her sketch. "I'm hopeless."

"No. You have talent."

She looked back and forth between Hugo's drawing and her own.

"You're just being kind," she said, but the word 'kind' sounded cold and flat.

"I mean it."

She studied Hugo for a long, quiet moment. He tried to see past the dark shields of her eyes, but he couldn't reach the woman behind them.

She extended her hand and said, "Frances Webster. Frankie."

Her handshake was aggressive.

"Frankie," he said. "Hugo Strauss."

She turned her attention back to the model.

Hugo let the silence continue but he was pleased. She had begun the conversation.

Gary descended on them occasionally.

He complimented Hugo: "The Arts may be winning."

On one of his circuits, he took the charcoal from Frankie's hand and redrew one of her lines.

"Don't hold yourself back," he said. "Let it flow."

Good advice, Hugo thought.

A few minutes after Gary had left, Hugo said, "He's right."

She looked at him but didn't respond.

"Don't worry about the result," he said.

Her eyes narrowed, as if he had insulted her. "I'm not worried."

He didn't want her to be angry at him.

"Good," he said, lamely.

They didn't speak to each other again.

When the class ended, they walked out together.

"Goodnight, Frankie," Hugo said. "See you next week."

"Goodnight," she said, without looking at him.

That night, Hugo couldn't fall asleep. He finally went down to the studio, took out a pad and a piece of charcoal and began to draw Frankie's face. When he finished, he thought he had captured not only her features, but her mood: tense, alert. Defensive, maybe.

He had included the two tiny holes in her earlobe. He wondered why she didn't wear earrings to class. Not the first time. Not tonight. Did she ever wear earrings? At work? On dates?

What kind of earring would match the structure of her face? The curve of her cheekbones? Her attitude? Her style?

Hugo walked out of the studio into a short, narrow hallway and opened the door at the end of it. He switched on the light.

This was his mother's workshop. A jeweler's bench. Every tool a craftsman would ever need.

His mother had created beauty here. Designs that were admired and imitated. That had started trends, set standards.

There was a bookshelf in the corner of the room. He took two scrapbooks off the shelf, one much thicker than the other. He switched off the light in the workshop and went back into the studio.

Hugo sat down at the work table and placed the two scrapbooks on it, the thicker one, his mother's, on top of the other, his.

He played a lyrical Thelonius Monk recording of Duke Ellington's songs. As he listened, he rested his hands on the scrapbooks, his fingers lightly beating time to the music.

Her visions. My visions.

He opened his mother's scrapbook and leafed through it. It was a fertile seedbed of ideas and images: photographs and drawings of seashells, flowers, rock formations, miscellaneous shapes; preliminary sketches of jewelry designs; even fragments of poetry ("the sessions of sweet, silent thought"). Her visual imagination, her artistry, were apparent on every page. You could trace the lifelines of some of her finished designs, sketch by sketch, from gestation through uncertain childhood to confident maturity.

Hugo closed her scrapbook, set it aside, and opened his own.

There are good ideas here, too, aren't there?

There were. But not as many.

His images usually came to life slowly, painfully. Often, they miscarried. But he was pleased with many of them. Proud of a few. Most had never been transformed into jewelry.

"You learned the craft, but not the art."

For years, though he didn't want to believe his mother's cold appraisal of him, he didn't have the courage to disprove it. Now he would try. Not out in the marketplace. Not yet. Here. In his mother's workshop, where no one would know if he failed.

And he may have already chosen his first project.

I could design a pair of earrings for Frankie. The perfect pair for her.

They could speak for him. Tell her how he felt, if it turned out that he had feelings for her.

And at the same time, perhaps he could make his mother's workshop his own.

VIII

Hugo thought of himself as a "nominal" Jew. Both his parents were Jewish, but neither of them believed in a Divine Being or attended services or performed holiday rituals.

Hugo's father said, "If there *is* a God, he's got a whole universe to take care of. Billions and billions of stars and planets. You think he's worried about a bunch of little worms like us?"

His mother said, "Please don't sentence me to Heaven. All the most interesting people—all my *friends*—will be in Hell."

Hugo hadn't been bar mitzvahed.

As he told Jamie, "I have a truce with God. We stay out of each other's way."

This year, Hanukkah arrived three weeks before Christmas. Caroline, a Lutheran, once asked him why the Jewish holidays seemed to begin on a different date every year.

Hugo's explanation was far from definitive.

"The Jews have a lunar calendar, I think. Everybody else uses a solar calendar. They don't match."

Caroline asked, "Why don't the Jews switch?"

"Tradition?"

Hugo's grandparents on his mother's side were Orthodox and her brother Myron stayed in the fold, keeping the faith and a Kosher home, but relaxing into Reform Judaism. He and Esther felt duty-bound to invite Hugo to a Seder every Passover, a dinner on the first nights of Hanukkah and Rosh Hashanah, and a breaking-the-fast meal after sundown on Yom Kippur, even though Hugo never fasted.

Vivian, Myron and Esther's daughter, usually came to the holiday dinners. Years ago, when their son Geoffrey still lived in Connecticut, he and his family used to come, too. And without fail, he and Myron celebrated with a bitter political argument. When Geoffrey moved to Seattle, the holiday spirit was restored.

Caroline had enjoyed Esther's holiday dinners—chicken soup with matzo balls, brisket, potato pancakes, noodle pudding, sweet red wine. And she sat through the minimal ceremonies on each occasion like a tolerant anthropologist observing a primitive tribe.

She and Hugo had been married by a minister. She attended church with her parents on an occasional Sunday and at Christmas and Easter. Hugo stayed home.

Two years after she and Hugo got married, Caroline's parents, who were high school teachers, retired and moved to Asheville, North Carolina. They had five children and Caroline, their youngest, was their least favorite. They called her once a week and visited now and then but, in the absence of grandchildren, usually kept their distance.

Caroline didn't mind. They weren't part of her plan.

As the youngest member of the family ("the kid," Myron called him), Hugo lit the first Hanukkah candle. Vivian said the prayers. By mutual agreement, they exchanged cards, not presents. But Myron, respecting the tradition of giving money (Hanukkah *gelt*) to children, insisted on giving Vivian and Hugo a dollar each.

The meal, as always, was a treat.

"The brisket is great," Hugo said, and he meant it.

"Vivian made the noodle pudding," Esther observed, proudly.

"Also great," Hugo added.

"No big deal," Vivian said, with a wan smile. "You follow the recipe."

"Viv, you going away this year?" Myron asked.

Vivian nodded. "Turks and Caicos."

"You're going to Turkey?" Esther said. "That's not a safe place for Jews."

Vivian laughed. "Not Turkey, Mom. *Turks and Caicos*. They're islands. In the West Indies, south of the Bahamas. Very nice resort area."

"I never heard of them," Esther said.

It was Myron's turn to laugh. "Sounds like a Yiddish curse."

"Are you going *with* somebody?" Esther asked.

"A friend."

That wasn't enough information for Esther.

"What *kind* of friend?"

"A *good* friend," Vivian said, pretending not to get the point.

"Vivian..."

"All right, Mom," Vivian relented. "A *male friend*. Unmarried. A lawyer. Makes a great living. Good looking. And he'd rather die a painful death than get married."

Esther sighed dramatically and said, "Have a good time."

"We will, Mom."

After a few minutes of silent chewing, Myron broke the silence.

"Hugo, how many classes you been to?"

"Just two. There's a break now. Gary's going to the Caribbean."

"To Turkeys and Whatsis?" Myron asked and chuckled.

"I don't know where he's going," Hugo said.

"So the term is over?" Esther asked.

"He doesn't work that way," Hugo said. "People come and go."

"Are you learning anything?" Vivian asked.

"For me, it's more like *remembering* things."

"Is he a good teacher?" Myron wondered.

"Better than I expected."

"Are you thinking more now about—what we talked about?" Myron asked.

"Yes."

Myron smiled and reached across the table to pat Hugo's shoulder.

"*Only* thinking about it," Hugo added, but Myron kept smiling.

IX

Over the next few weeks, during the holiday rush, Myron kept the store open until ten every day, including Sunday. He often asked Hugo to double as a salesman.

But no matter how busy the day, Hugo spent two or three hours every night with his scrapbook and sketch pad, examining his past design ideas, evaluating them, reshaping them, searching for a new synthesis.

He couldn't tell you what he was searching for, but he hoped that he would recognize it.

His mother had often custom-designed a piece for a customer, but Hugo never had. So he started to practice, matching customers who came into the store with designs in his scrapbook.

A woman was shopping for her daughter, a slim, graceful girl, who clearly didn't enjoy being the center of attention.

That narrow gold necklace, dozens of tiny, overlapping oak leaves. It would be perfect for her.

His mother would have said, "You should have taken it a step further. Why are all the leaves the same size and shape?"

She would have drawn a different design. Freer. More dramatic.

He understood her approach. It reflected her spirit. But he didn't like it as much as his own, which reflected *his* spirit.

A well-dressed, elderly man wanted to surprise his wife with a brooch. He said she loved pearls.

The blackened silver oyster shell with a large pearl suspended in it.

His mother would have called it "pleasant, but uninspired." Myron loved it. Joe Berger's shop produced it. And people bought it.

A young couple wanted matching friendship rings.

Two delicate hands clasped tightly to form a slim gold ring.

His mother would have called it "unimaginative, unexciting." Myron loved the design. And couples bought it.

If Frankie came into the store to buy a pair of earrings, what would he show her?

He toyed with several of his designs, tried to improve them, but they didn't reflect her face, or what he thought was her style.

Then he discovered the seed of an idea that showed promise. He had clipped a photograph of a white Easter Lily, a long, tubular flower, pointed at the base and flaring to a wide mouth. He had sketched it several times, each time eliminating some of the details, until it began to evolve into a more abstract shape. But he had abandoned it.

Now he refined the design, creating a sharper curve in it to match the shape of Frankie's face, the aggressive slant of her cheekbones. He reduced the petals to fine lines engraved on the surface. The flower had been transformed into the essence of a flower.

He drew the earring from several different angles, completing it with a wire hook at the narrow end.

He gave the design a final test by adding it to his drawing of Frankie. He thought it would fit her perfectly.

But that was only the first step.

He knew he had to be cautious. He couldn't give her an expensive gift, a pair of gold or silver earrings. That would be too much too soon. She might be offended.

He would choose an inexpensive material. A metal that was easy to work with, easy to bend into shape. Niobium.

And then, remembering the rainbow brooch Frankie had worn, he thought he should add color to the earrings.

Not the color of a lily. The color of spring: green. She'd probably like that.

With a felt-tip pen, he filled in the color.

The drawing reminded Hugo that Frankie had *two* pierced holes in her earlobe. He should design a second piece.

Low-key. Simple. Not competing with the earring. A plain stone mounted on a stud. Fastened with three or four prongs.

The earring was green, so he would use malachite. Also inexpensive. A green gem with mysterious, curling streaks of dark green and yellow green.

Hugo added the stud to his drawing.

What would his mother say about the design?

Too inhibited. Too conservative. Let yourself go! Break the rules!

He didn't agree. He thought the earrings would be perfect for Frankie.

And now that he had designed them, he wondered, *Will I ever make them? Will she ever wear them?*

The answer to the first question was Yes. He didn't know the answer to the second.

X

Hugo spent this New Year's Eve alone.

I wonder what Frankie's doing tonight. Is she with someone she's in love with? Friends? Family?

Thinking back over all his New Year's Eves, there wasn't much worth remembering. Before Caroline, he went through the usual motions with his current girlfriend, drinking too much, pretending that one night of the year mattered more than any other.

When Hugo was a teenager, when he was sixteen, seventeen, eighteen, his parents took New Year's Eve sailing vacations to the Caribbean for two or three weeks. Without him. He would stay at Jamie's house.

When he met Caroline, they spent quiet New Year's Eves together, at first with Jamie and Louise. Caroline's father was an alcoholic, so heavy drinking was not on the agenda. Hugo didn't really care. Eventually, Jamie and Louise decided to spend the night with other friends.

Last New Year's Eve, he had been dating a clinical psychologist, Cheryl Altman, for four or five months. He found her attractive and they had a good time together. But his silence displeased her. She tried to cure it.

Hugo told Jamie, "She wants to *solve* me."

Cheryl the Solver asked Hugo lots of questions, speaking very slowly, enunciating carefully, as if he were a confused child. He could almost hear the gears turning in her psychologist's brain, analyzing every word, every nuance.

"You said your parents...were famous?"

"Yes."

"How...did that make you...feel?"

"Like someone with famous parents."

Cheryl laughed and said, "Seriously."

"I am serious."

"Did you...envy them? Resent them?"

"No."

"Hugo. Don't hide...from me."

This was a game he didn't enjoy playing. And Cheryl kept trying to win.

They ate Thai food, welcomed the New Year together, kissed and coupled in the guest room.

In the darkness, when Hugo felt at peace with himself and the visible universe, Cheryl the Solver said, "Tell me about your mother and father."

"Nothing to tell."

"Lots to tell."

"Not now," Hugo said.

Cheryl kissed his mouth, his cheek, his shoulder. He felt the soft mounds of her breasts, her belly.

"You don't talk, Hugo. You never tell me...anything."

"Nothing to tell."

"Bullshit!"

She sat up in bed, leaned over him.

"Your parents are dead," she said. "When...did they die?"

"Why do you care?"

"I want to know you. *Really* know you."

Hugo looked up at her looming shadow in the darkness.

"I was twenty-two."

"They died together?"

"A sailing accident," he said. "In a storm."

But he didn't tell her his fantasy: that they hadn't died. That they had sailed away to start a new life, in a new place, so they could be rid of him.

"When you were twenty-two," Cheryl said.

"Yes."

"You got married when you were twenty-three."

"Yes."

"Does that tell you something?" she asked.

"No."

"Think about it."

"I want to go to sleep," Hugo said.

She sighed and lay down again.

"Silence is...unhealthy," she said.

"Go to sleep."

"You have to face...who you are. Who they were...to you."

He didn't answer her.

Later that week, he broke up with her.

Hugo had brought his mother's workshop back to life.

He tested the ventilator: it worked perfectly, but he had to replace the filter. He bought a new set of blades for the jeweler's saw; a tank of oxygen and one of acetylene to feed the soldering iron; flux, polishing compounds, emery boards; and a bottle of ammonium sulfate, the electrolyte solution that would add color to Frankie's earrings.

Without telling Myron, he also purchased a thin sheet of niobium and two very small, matching malachite stones in a shape that jewelers call a *cabochon,* flat-bottomed and curved on top.

He had made a detailed drawing of the earring to scale, then a template—an exact outline of the piece that he would cut and shape to form each earring.

He was ready to begin. And he decided to start on New Year's Eve, as a celebration of the future.

For dinner that night, he picked up an order of veal marsala, linguine and garlic bread at the Venezia Ristorante in Fairfield Center. He opened a bottle of Chianti and ate in the den, watching tedious New Year's Eve hi-jinks on television.

At about ten o'clock, Hugo turned off the television, put his dish and utensils into the dishwasher and transferred the wine bottle and empty glass to the work table in the studio.

Then he entered the workshop, turned on the bright lamp that illuminated the jeweler's bench, and sat down. All the materials were waiting for him. The niobium sheet. His drawing of the template. A pad of tracing paper. A steel ruler. A jeweler's saw. A scribe—a steel rod with a sharp needle at the end, for marking a pattern on metal.

He sat there motionless, minute after minute, ready to begin. But he didn't begin.

This isn't my place yet, he thought. *It's still hers.*

His mother's image was burned into his memory: beautiful, distant, so deeply engaged with her thoughts, her art, her husband, that whenever he talked to her, he felt he was intruding. His father was openly dismissive, but she was seductive, elusive, a magical mirage who disappeared when he approached her.

That hadn't changed. He was still intimidated by a woman who had died ten years ago.

And I've designed a pair of earrings for a woman I don't even know.

Hugo traced the drawing of the template. Then he cut out the traced pattern. With the steel ruler and the scribe, he slowly, painstakingly transferred the outline of the pattern to the niobium sheet. Twice.

It was exacting, exhausting work.

He took a break. He went back into the studio, poured himself a glass of wine and listened to a Mozart sonata for two pianos, a sunny, free-flowing river of melody.

It was so easy for Mozart, so natural, Hugo thought. *Both the art and the craft.*

After an hour or so, he returned to the workshop.

He examined the sheet of metal he had marked but decided that was all he could do tonight.

He returned to the den with the bottle of Chianti and turned on the television. It was past midnight. He watched a frenetic singing group he had never heard of, a comedian who was almost funny, and a late-night host who kept exchanging insults with his bandleader.

At 1:40, he said *Goodnight* to the late-night host and turned off the television.

His next drawing class was in three days.

That's when I'll ask Frankie to go out.

XI

At the beginning of the class, Gary (tanned by the Caribbean sun) said, "I hope we all have a happy, healthy, *creative* New Year."

The class responded with a ragged chorus of "Happy New Year!"

Hugo thought the model was an ideal subject: she was a plump, big-breasted woman, an anthology of hills and valleys, light and shadow.

He positioned himself next to Frankie. She was wearing black again and a color-splashed scarf, but no earrings.

"Hi, Frankie."

"Hugo."

She didn't look happy.

He took a chance.

"You okay?"

She didn't answer him.

They began to draw. Hugo could see that she was holding the charcoal too tightly and she moved it across the page just as tightly. The lines she drew were cramped and uncomfortable.

Frankie glanced at Hugo's sketch, frowned and said, "I can't do this. I don't belong here."

"You do."

"I'm just trying to get myself started again," she said, almost whispering.

"Started?"

Frankie shook her head. "It's a long story. Too long."

Hugo didn't want her to leave the class.

"I can help," he said.

Her answer was a doubtful look.

"If you'll let me," he added.

"Private lessons at your place?" Frankie asked, as if she'd been offered that kind of help before.

"No. Right here. Now."

"What can *you* do that Gary can't?" she wondered.

"I'll show you."

Frankie shrugged. "Okay," she said.

"Let me guide you," Hugo said.

He got behind her. "Just relax."

She looked over her shoulder at him, still uncertain.

He reached out, closed his fingers over her wrist. He felt the muscles in her arm push back against him.

"Relax," he said.

She took a deep breath and he felt most of the tension dissipate.

He was very close to her. He could smell her perfume, a delicate, not-too-sweet scent. And he could feel the heat of her body.

"Look at the model's hip," Hugo said.

He paused.

"The shape of it."

He paused again.

"The line of it."

Pause.

"Remember the line."

Pause.

"Remember it," Hugo said. "Now we'll draw it."

She let him guide her hand. The charcoal drew a sensuous curve.

Frankie smiled, the first smile Hugo had seen.

The smile faded quickly.

"But I can't do that without you," she said.

Hugo let go of her wrist and returned to his own easel.

"You can."

Her look was a little softer. A little less guarded.

"Trust yourself," Hugo said.

She looked at the line they had drawn.

"Turn lines into shapes," he said. "Make mistakes. Do too much. Not too little."

She thought about what he had said. Then she began to draw.

He worked on his own sketch, looking over at her occasionally. She was still tense at first, still too tight. Then, gradually, he saw her loosening the chains, taking chances. The lines she drew were longer, freer. She began to turn them into shapes. She made mistakes, but now they were what Hugo told her were the right kind of mistakes: big ones, not small ones.

Once, when he looked at her, she smiled at him and nodded.

When Gary critiqued her first drawing of the evening, he said, "Now you're getting the idea. Keep it up."

He winked at Hugo and, silently, his lips formed the word "Thanks."

For the rest of the evening, Frankie alternated smiles and frowns, fluctuating between satisfaction and frustration.

At the end of the class, Hugo walked out with her.

"There are other things I can show you," he said.

"Next class."

"Yes. Basic forms. Spheres. Cylinders. As a framework."

"What if I'm hopeless?" Frankie asked, wistfully.

"You're not."

"We'll see," she said, a delicate trace of warmth in her voice.

"Like to stop for a drink?"

"A drink?"

"It's early," he said.

Frankie seemed to be considering the possibility.

Finally, she asked, "Where?"

"Where do you live?"

"Fairfield."

"Me, too. You know Maxine's?"

"On Reef Road?"

"Yes."

"I've passed it," she said.

"It's quiet."

Frankie studied the moon's shivering reflection in the dark, churning water of the Sound.

"I don't know if I'm in the mood," she said.

"My treat," Hugo teased.

An icy wind wrapped itself around them.

"All right," she said. "I'll meet you there."

Hugo reached Maxine's first.

The restaurant was divided by a long, curved bar. To the left of it was a narrow cocktail lounge. To the right, a large dining room. Hugo picked a table in the lounge.

It was a few minutes after ten o'clock on a Wednesday night. There were only a handful of people at the bar and, in the dining room, one foursome finishing a late dinner. An Elton John album was playing in the background.

A waitress started to approach him, but Hugo waved her off, pointing to the empty chair across from him.

As the minutes ticked by, he wondered if Frankie had changed her mind. Maybe she was on her way home.

Will she disappoint me? he thought.

Something about her had touched him. Deeply. He didn't know what it was.

Unless he was fooling himself. Unless she was another seductive mirage who would disappear when he got too close to her.

Will I disappoint her?

Assuming she was interested in him. An unlikely assumption.

When Frankie arrived, she seemed uncomfortable. She sat down at the table and unbuttoned her coat, but didn't take it off.

"I thought you changed your mind," Hugo said.

"I almost did."

The waitress came over.

"What can I get you?"

Hugo waited for Frankie to order.

"Beer, I guess," she said.

"Stella for me," Hugo said.

"Okay," Frankie said.

The waitress reviewed the order, "Two Stellas," and added, "We close at eleven."

After the waitress left, Hugo asked, "How long have you been in the class?"

"A couple of weeks before you started."

"Gary hasn't helped?"

Frankie shook her head and said, "You taught me more tonight than he has."

"Did you let him teach you?"

She smiled. "Maybe not."

Her smiles, so rare, softened the taut lines of her face.

That's all it takes to make her beautiful.

"You should let him," Hugo said.

"You're an artist?" Frankie asked.

"I'm in the jewelry business."

"Selling?"

"Repairing. Selling sometimes. I used to design."

"Why did you stop?"

Hugo shrugged and said, "I'm designing again."

The waitress returned, poured a glass for each of them, left the check on the table and retreated.

Hugo raised his glass and said, "To good mistakes."

Frankie smiled, clinked her glass against his and they savored a first shared taste of the beer.

"What do you do?" Hugo asked. "Your job, I mean."

"Nothing exciting. I write marketing copy for web sites. Freelance. Mostly for small companies."

"So you're a writer."

"Small 'w'," Frankie said. "But I'm trying to get back to *real* writing."

"Stories? Novels?"

"Yes."

"Why did you stop?"

She smiled at the echo of her question to him.

"Lots of reasons," she said.

Hugo wanted to reach across the table and stroke her hair, her beautiful, gray-streaked hair. He wanted to make her smile. To kiss her beautiful smile. To smell her perfume and feel her heat again.

"You didn't want to come here tonight?" he asked.

"I haven't been socializing much."

"Too many terrible dates?"

A long pause.

Then softly, "Phil and I split about a year ago. A bad divorce after a bad marriage. I'm not in a hurry to meet anybody."

Don't rush her.

"I was married, too," Hugo said. "My wife died."

"Sorry."

"Three years ago."

"You must miss her."

Don't tell her the truth, whatever that is.

"Seems like another world. Long ago."

"I wish I could say the same about *my* marriage," she said.

They drank quietly for a minute or two.

"Why did you take Gary's class?" Frankie asked.

"A refresher course. Why did you?"

"I'm trying something new," she said. "Trying to get into a creative mood again. And to start getting out again."

Hugo smiled. "Getting out, but not *going* out?"

"For now."

"Glad to oblige."

Frankie enjoyed that remark.

Hugo raised his glass and said, "To not dating."

Frankie laughed and said, "Hear, hear!"

"For now," Hugo added.

After a pause, he asked, "Where in Fairfield do you live?"

"The condos near Blackrock Turnpike."

"I'm across from Fairfield University."

"A very nice neighborhood," she said.

"I grew up in that house."

I wonder if that sounds strange. Never leaving home.

"Gary said your parents were artists?"

"My mother designed jewelry. Very successful."

"And your father?"

"A painter. Portraits, for people with money. Lots of other paintings for himself. Also very successful."

"Talent on both sides," Frankie said.

"Guess so."

"I wasn't that lucky," she said. "My Mom and Dad owned a bakery. He went to work in the middle of the night. For as long as I can remember."

"Work at night. Sleep during the day?"

"Right. My brother, too. When my father died, my brother took over the bakery."

"And you're a writer."

"The first in the family. Who knows why?"

"Does it matter?"

"No. I answer to no one. As the baker's daughter, my motto is, *Let 'em eat cake!*"

Frankie laughed at her own joke.

There was an awkward silence and she finished her glass of beer too quickly.

"Thanks for the invitation," she said. "I'm sorry to leave so soon but I'm tired, ready to call it a night. I've got this big assignment to do tomorrow."

She stood up and buttoned her coat.

"See you next week," she said.

"Next week."

"Good night, Hugo."

"Good night, Frankie."

Hugo stayed at Maxine's until eleven. He had time to order another beer. To think about Frankie. For the rest of the night.

XII

The next night, like virtually every Thursday night, Jamie's wife Louise set up two card tables in their basement rec room and played Bridge with a group of friends. On those nights, Jamie had an open invitation at Hugo's place to drink beer, munch on potato chips/Fritos and watch sports or a Netflix movie.

Tonight, they picked a super-hero film, kept the sound low, and talked through it.

Jamie looked worried.

"What's the problem?" Hugo asked.

"Lately, Sean" (his eight-year-old son) "is screwing up at school."

"His marks?"

"No, he's doing okay in class. He keeps getting into fights. Talks back to teachers."

"You know why?"

"No," Jamie said. "We had to go see his guidance counselor. She asked *us* why."

"Big help."

"Louise is really pissed off."

"Sure."

"She runs a pretty tight ship," Jamie said.

"Too tight? For the kids?"

Jamie shrugged. "Could be."

For a few minutes, they watched one of the super-heroes battle a satanic super-enemy.

"Are you happy?" Hugo asked.

Jamie considered the question for a minute or so.

"I guess so," he said. "I mean, for one thing, I love my job."

"Really?"

Jamie smiled and said, "I know it's hard for you to believe."

"Filling out tax returns?"

Jamie shook his head.

"These aren't your simple-shit personal returns," he said. "We've got branches in thirty-six countries. You have to understand the tax laws in all of them. It's like putting together a thousand-piece jigsaw puzzle."

"That's exciting?"

Jamie laughed. "Anyway," he said, "I'm happy at work."

"And at home?" Hugo asked.

"Usually."

"Not always?"

"Nobody is *always* happy. We have a good marriage. But she worries about *everything*. It can be...tiring."

"Yeah."

"I love my kids. They have their problems, but I guess that's what life is about."

"You hear from Barney?" Hugo asked.

"He called a couple of times. Moaned a little. The divorce is on track."

"He'll be better off."

"I guess so."

Jamie watched one of the movie villains blow up an entire city while Hugo opened a second round of beers.

"What about you?" Jamie asked. "Are you happy?"

"Not really. But not unhappy."

"Where the hell does that leave you?"

"In between."

"How come?" Jamie asked. "Since Caroline died, you've been dating some interesting women. You're having a good time, aren't you? Doesn't that make you happy?"

"No."

"And I've been envying you!"

After a pause, Hugo said, "I've met someone."

"Who?"

"In drawing class."

"What's her name?"

"Frances. Calls herself Frankie."

"Is she an artist?"

"No," Hugo said. "A writer."

"Keep talking."

"Not much to tell. Yet."

"Have you gone out with her?"

"Drinks after class. Yesterday."

"I'm listening," Jamie said.

"She's divorced. Lives in town. Don't know much more."

"And you think she's special?"

"Yes."

"Why?"

Hugo wished he could answer that question.

"I'm not sure," he said.

"Oh, sweet mystery of love..."

Hugo laughed.

"She's got me back to designing," he said.

"It's about time."

"Making jewelry. For her."

"Very romantic."

"In my mother's workshop."

Jamie raised his arms and shouted, "Hallelujah!"

"Frankie doesn't know."

"What are you making?" Jamie asked.

"Earrings."

"Can I see them?"

Hugo hesitated.

"They're not finished," he said, "but I'll show you."

Hugo switched off the television and led Jamie into the workshop.

His drawings of the earrings and the studs were on the jeweler's bench.

"This is the design," he said.

The drawing of Frankie's face was also on the bench.

"That's her," Hugo said.

Jamie appraised both the jewelry and Frankie.

"Very nice. They'll look great on her," he said.

"Hope so."

Hugo picked up a miniature fluted metal tube from the bench and showed it to Jamie.

"Interesting," Jamie said. "Is that silver?"

Hugo shook his head.

"Niobium."

"Never heard of it."

"Not pricey," Hugo said. "Easy to work with."

Jamie looked at the drawings again and asked, "How are you going to make them green? Some kind of special paint?"

"No. Electric current. Different voltages give you different colors."

"No shit?"

"No shit."

"I'd better stick to filling out tax returns," Jamie said.

Hugo laughed.

"Do you think *she'll* make you happy?" Jamie asked.

"Wish I knew," Hugo said.

During the next class, Hugo tutored Frankie again. She was more at ease with him.

"I'll never be an artist," she said, "but I'm starting to enjoy myself here."

"Good."

"More important: I've got a short story in the works!" She smiled at him as if he had a right to share in her happiness.

"Great," Hugo said.

"I'm a little rusty," Frankie added, "but I'm on my way."

"We should celebrate."

"A beer at Maxine's?"

Hugo shook his head and said, "How about dinner?"

"It's too late for that, isn't it?"

"Not tonight. Friday."

Gary interrupted them.

He examined her drawing.

"Big improvement," Gary said. "Am I making a difference, or is it Hugo?"

"Both of you," Frankie said, diplomatically.

"I don't mind sharing," Gary said. "May I make some suggestions?"

"Please do."

He spent a few minutes with Frankie, showed her the effect of a horizon line, demonstrated cross-hatched shading and asked her to apply both to her next sketch.

He patted Hugo on the shoulder and moved on.

Hugo wanted to continue his conversation with Frankie, but she was working on a new drawing.

She's not sure if she wants to go out with me. I'll let her think about it.

He had almost finished her earrings. (She wasn't wearing any tonight, as usual.) He only had to add the color. And make the studs. But he still didn't know if, or when, he would give them to her.

A half hour had passed before Hugo asked, "How about dinner? Friday."

She looked at him but didn't answer.

"Or Saturday," he said.

After a brief pause, she said, "Friday is fine."

"Pick you up at seven-thirty?"

She nodded.

"Any restaurant you like."

"You pick it," she said.

"Allergic to anything?" Hugo asked.

Frankie smiled and answered, "Tex-Mex."

"Beans kill me, too," he said.

They both laughed at that.

XIII

The next morning at the store, Myron couldn't stop pacing.

"You're coming to dinner tonight." he said.

"I haven't been invited."

"Consider yourself invited."

"I'm not sure..."

Myron shook his head. "You're sure."

"What's wrong?"

"Geoffrey is staying with us for a couple of days," Myron said.

"Just him?"

"Just him. He left the family at home. He's giving a talk at Yale."

"Very nice," Hugo said.

"Esther is in Heaven. I think she levitated yesterday."

"And you?"

Myron sighed. "We haven't argued yet."

"So you don't need me."

Myron almost shouted, "I do!"

"Okay," Hugo said, although he had intended to finish Frankie's earrings that night. "I'll be there."

Geoffrey was slender and soft-spoken, but not shy. To Hugo, he always seemed distracted, as if he were listening to a radio broadcast that only he could hear.

"Geoffrey was *invited* to Yale," Esther said, proudly. "*Invited* to give a talk."

"I'm on a panel, Mom," Geoffrey corrected.

Esther ignored that distinction.

"Invited," she repeated.

"I'll be talking about the program I started a couple of years ago," Geoffrey said. "My 'Ace' program."

"Ace?" Esther wondered.

"Short for Art Access and Education," Geoffrey said.

He shifted into lecture mode. "We wanted to find a way to interest kids in art. Especially those who don't normally go to museums. Inner city kids and kids in small towns and rural areas."

"Good idea," Hugo said.

"We're operating on two tracks," Geoffrey said. "First, we bring students to the museums. And we provide everything—guided tours, information packages, and lunch, too—with local businesses picking up the tab."

"Wonderful," Esther murmured.

Hugo watched her face when she looked at her son. The warmth of her smile. Her eyes admiring him.

Hugo had never seen that look in his mother's eyes.

"And on the second track, we bring the museums to the kids. A real painting or two and the rest in slide presentations at schools, libraries, community centers."

"Getting results?" Hugo asked.

"In some places. In the cities, we're making real progress with black and Latino kids. They're catching on. I've given some of these talks and I can *feel* their interest. Their energy. But in the small towns, mostly white kids: not much reaction."

"Why do you think that is?" Esther asked.

"More stew, Mom?"

She served him a massive second serving.

Geoffrey forked up and, with pleasure, devoured a healthy mouthful.

"I think city kids are more open to experience," he said. "The small-towners are narrower. Less curious about the world. Locked into the way they live."

Hugo waited for Myron to say something. Anything. But throughout the meal, his uncle maintained an attentive silence, grunting and nodding his head occasionally.

Geoffrey kept one eye on Myron, as if he were hoping for an argument to begin. But Myron simply met his son's intense gaze with a placid, almost haughty smile.

Dessert was (of course) Geoffrey's favorite: freshly baked blueberry pie with vanilla ice cream.

As Geoffrey consumed the pie, oohing and aahing to please his mother, Myron finally spoke.

"I was cleaning out the attic a couple of days ago," he said. "I found a box of old photographs. Very old. Interesting stuff."

He got up from the table, left the dining room and came back a minute or so later with a batch of pictures.

He sat down again, cradling the photos in his hands.

"Lots of shots of Mom and you and your sister," he said to Geoffrey.

"Suitable for blackmail, I bet," Geoffrey said, with a frown.

Esther disagreed. "You were a beautiful child."

Geoffrey smiled. "To you, maybe."

She reached across the table and stroked his hair.

Myron began handing photographs to Esther, who enjoyed each of them noisily before she passed it to Geoffrey. He hardly looked at any of the pictures, turning them over to Hugo as quickly as he could.

Hugo examined the photos politely, smiling occasionally, before he gave them back to Myron.

When there was only one picture left, Myron said, "This one is for you, Hugo."

"For me?"

"It's of you and your mother when you were a baby."

For as long as he could remember, Hugo's mother wouldn't allow anyone to take her picture.

"I don't need frozen memories," she said. "The past is dead. The only time that matters is now."

His father let her make the rules. He painted portraits for a living, but there were no photos in the house. No albums.

Myron handed him the photograph, a faded black-and-white scene: Hugo's mother sitting in the studio with a five- or six-month old baby on her lap. She was holding the baby away from her body, as if she were about to give it to someone else. Her expression—challenging, aggressive—was familiar, but he had never seen her like this before. His mother had shoulder-length blond hair. The woman in the picture had dark hair, cut very short. His mother's face and figure showed how much she enjoyed food and hated exercise. The woman in the picture was slim, her face taut and angular.

But there was something else about her image that made him more than uneasy, that frightened him.

The woman in the picture looked like Frankie.

Late that night, Hugo sat in the studio, drinking wine and studying the faded black-and-white photograph Myron had given him. He was calmer now, but still uneasy.

When he had taken a closer look at the woman's face, his mother's face, the resemblance to Frankie was less specific, more generic.

But did I see my Mom's face when I saw Frankie?

The woman in the photograph stared at him, challenged him, held him the way she held her baby, tightly, possessively, without embracing him.

Is that why I'm attracted to Frankie?

Was the woman in the photograph mocking him? Trying to make him feel like a foolish child again?

He could almost hear her voice: "Frankie is your second chance to be loved by me."

But I'm not a child.

Maybe he couldn't think of Frankie in quite the same way again. That didn't mean the woman in the photograph was right.

But he had to be certain that Frankie wasn't just an echo of his past. Because until he was sure—*unless* he was sure—he wouldn't let himself fall in love with her.

XIV

Frankie's apartment was spacious and neatly furnished. But to Hugo it felt more like a hotel room than a home. The magazines and books were too neatly shelved. There were no art works on display. There wasn't a trace of idiosyncrasy or personality.

And there were no family photos in sight.

Is she like Mom, someone who doesn't want to remember her past?

Frankie looked lovely. She wore a flowing, ankle-length black skirt and a crisp white blouse. A silk scarf added bright splashes of color. There was a tiny flower, a delicately sculptured rose, clipped to her hair. (And she wasn't wearing earrings.)

She seemed uncomfortable, almost shy.

Not at all like Mom, he thought, and that was reassuring.

Frankie asked him if he would like a glass of wine.

"I've had a head start," she said. "I may be a little nervous."

"Relax," Hugo said.

He silently gave himself the same advice.

She smiled. "Okay."

"Wine sounds fine."

He followed her into the living room. On the coffee table were a bottle of Pinot Noir and two glasses, one half-full. She filled his glass, handed it to him and refilled her own.

"Please sit down," she said.

He sat on the couch and she sat down near him but not next to him.

He raised his glass.

"Cheers," he said, but the word sounded hollow to him and far from cheerful.

She touched his glass with hers.

After he had sampled the wine he said, "It's an eight o'clock reservation. San Moritz."

"I've been there. It's a nice place."

"It is," Hugo said.

She wasn't looking at him when she said, "Since the divorce, a little more than a year now, I haven't gone out on a *date*."

She made the word "date" sound almost sinister.

"I understand."

She shook her head and said, "I wasn't just hurt, I was angry. I still am."

Hugo wanted to comfort her but he couldn't find the words.

"At me, too?" he asked.

She sipped her wine pensively before she answered.

"No, not at you," she said, almost too softly to hear.

But she's sorry she's on a date.

Although they were sitting close to each other, Hugo felt as if they were far apart.

He wanted to tell her how beautiful she was. But he didn't.

He tried to let the silence ease the tension between them.

"I've been drawing," she said, "practicing."

"Good. Writing, too?"

"Yes, I'm lucky," Frankie said. "I work at home most days. Make my own schedule. There's plenty of free time."

"You *are* lucky."

"Even so, sometimes I feel a little isolated," she admitted. "Gary's class was a way to connect."

"*We've* connected," Hugo said. "Haven't we?"

"We don't really know each other."

"We do," Hugo said and pointed at her. "You're a writer."

Frankie played along, pointing at Hugo. "You're in the jewelry business."

"Your father was a baker."

"Your parents were artists."

"Let 'em eat cake!" Hugo said.

Frankie laughed. "Yeah! Let 'em!"

"Tex-Mex is out."

"Beans are major trouble," she said.

"You're divorced."

"And your wife...passed away," Frankie said, softly.

He didn't respond at once, as if his silence was a sign of mourning.

Then he said, "See? We know a lot."

"In a way," she agreed.

Hugo wanted to continue the game.

"One question," he said.

"What do you want to know?"

"Your gray hair?" he asked.

"It runs in my family. The *women* in my family. Gray hair when we're in our twenties."

"*Streaks* of gray?"

Frankie laughed again.

"No," she said. "I'm the only one who came up with that."

"I like it," Hugo said.

"Thank you," Frankie said.

They finished their wine quietly, more comfortably.

"Shall we go?" she asked.

"We shall."

They drank another glass of wine at the restaurant before dinner.

"Do you have any brothers or sisters?" Frankie asked.

"No."

"So you had two artists all to yourself. Teaching you."

Hugo wondered how much he should tell her. Why not the truth? Or at least, some of the truth.

"Not really," he said.

"Even by example?" Frankie said.

"They were too busy," Hugo said.

"With their work?"

"With themselves," he said. "With each other."

"That must have been painful," Frankie said.

"Got used to it," he said.

"It's amazing what we get used to."

She seemed to be waiting for him to pursue the subject, so he asked, "You, too?"

"When I graduated from UConn," Frankie said, "I had to stay at home with my mother. She was sick. My father had died when I was in high school. My brother and sister helped out with money. But she had two kids to take care of. And he was working every night."

She paused, as if she were carefully selecting the memories she was willing to share.

"I was able to find some free-lance work," Frankie said, "through someone I knew in college. And little by little, working at home, I managed to add a few more clients."

"And take care of your mother."

Frankie nodded. "She was a good woman. I was never angry at her. It wasn't her fault. But I had to put my life on hold."

"For how long?"

"About two years. She died quietly. In her sleep."

Frankie sipped her wine.

"I *hope* Mom *was* sleeping," she said. "I hope she didn't wake up in the middle of the night, alone in the dark, afraid, knowing this was the end."

"I hope so, too."

"But I was so used to taking care of her—she was such a big part of my life—that I felt kind of empty after she was gone. It took me a while to shake that off."

"But you did."

"I did," Frankie said.

She lapsed into a silence that said, "Let's talk about something else."

"You're writing a short story?"

"Yes," she said. "I've finished the first draft."

"What's it about?"

Frankie frowned. "That's not an easy question to answer. Stories never sound like much when you try to explain them."

"Sure."

"Really, what matters isn't the story," she added, "but how you tell it."

What mattered to Hugo was what the story could tell him about Frankie.

She smiled and said, "Okay, why not?"

He waited for her to begin.

Frankie studied Hugo's face for a moment, as if she was still deciding whether she should trust him.

"It's called 'Olivia's Dress,'" she said. "Olivia is a woman in her late thirties. She's very cool and efficient. She's the office manager for a medical practice, four or five doctors, and it runs very smoothly because of her. She still lives with her parents, goes to church every Sunday. And she's been engaged to a nice guy for a couple of years. They'll get married one of these days, but they're not in a rush. She seems to be doing fine. But there's one thing that's bothering Olivia."

Frankie paused, drank some wine and continued.

"One of the doctors is getting married. And she's going to buy a new dress for the wedding. And although this doesn't seem very important to anyone else, she's agonizing over it. She goes to one store after another. She tries on dozens of dresses. She doesn't like any of them. She's getting frantic. And no one can figure out why she's acting so strangely."

Frankie paused again. She seemed reluctant to go on.

"She finally picks a dress, although it doesn't really satisfy her. At the wedding ceremony at the end of the story, she finally admits—only to herself, of course—that she's in love with the doctor. That she feels a passion for him that she's never felt for anyone or anything else. And she's certain she never will feel that way again."

"She never told him?"

"She's someone who keeps her emotions locked up inside her because she's so afraid of being hurt. And she'll bury this feeling, this passion, too."

Frankie drank the last of her wine and said, "That's the story."

"It's sad."

"For writers," she said, "happiness is boring."

"Ever write a happy ending?"

"Not lately."

When they said *Good Night* at her door, Hugo asked, "Before the class on Wednesday: dinner?"

Fankie nodded.

"We don't have to go out," she said. "I'll make dinner."

"But..."

"I want to. Don't worry, I'm a good cook."

"And baker, of course?"

She smiled and said, "You bet your ass I am."

"Okay."

"I had a good time tonight," Frankie said.

"Me, too."

Hugo leaned forward and kissed her cheek lightly.

"I'll see you Wednesday," he said.

"About five o'clock?"

"About five o'clock."

XV

Jamie called Hugo on Saturday morning.

"How did it go?" he asked.

"How did *what* go?"

"Very funny," Jamie said.

"My date with Frankie?"

"What else?"

Hugo paused for a beat or two.

"It was fine," he said.

Jamie snorted. "Fine? What the hell does that mean?"

"We had a good time."

"Smoking, drinking and carousing?"

"No carousing," Hugo said. "Eating. Drinking. Talking."

Jamie groaned. "How exciting."

"I enjoyed it."

"I get the feeling you're not that interested in her any more."

"I am," Hugo said.

"Something happen to cool you off?"

"No."

"I don't believe you," Jamie said.

"Nothing happened."

"Are you going to see her again?"

"She's cooking dinner," Hugo said. "Wednesday."

"That's a good sign, isn't it?"

"Yes."

Jamie sighed and said, "Once in a while, would it kill you to say three or four words in a row?"

"It might."

Jamie laughed.

"How many years have I been doing all the talking for both of us?"

"A long time."

"It's too late to quit now, I guess."

"Much too late," Hugo said.

"Listen, I'll see you Thursday. Maybe then you'll have more to say."

"Maybe," Hugo said. "Maybe not."

That Sunday afternoon at K-J's, Hugo tried to enjoy the football game and the beer and Kevin Kelly's stream of consciousness, but he couldn't.

"You not feelin' well?" Kevin asked.

"I'm fine."

"You don't look it."

"I'm tired," Hugo said.

Kevin grinned suggestively. "Big night last night?"

Hugo just nodded.

Kevin gave Hugo the thumbs up.

"Way to go," he said.

Hugo smiled with simulated pride and tried to watch the football game.

Later that day, working until 1:30 in the morning, he finished setting the green malachite stones in the studs. The set—earrings and studs—was complete.

He wanted to give it to Frankie. To tell her that he had created these earrings just for her, to please her, to reflect her beauty.

But he wasn't ready yet. He still didn't trust his feelings.

On Monday at the store, Myron was unusually quiet.

"Geoffrey still here?" Hugo asked.

"Till tomorrow."

"Aunt Esther's happy."

"Thank God somebody is," Myron said, wearily. "We finally had a big fight, Geoffrey and me."

"Politics?"

"Yeah. But it's always more than that."

"It is?"

"My son is very smart," Myron said. "Vivian is, too, but Esther never made such a big deal out of her. You know, Jewish mothers and their sons."

Not my *Jewish mother,* Hugo thought.

"When Geoffrey went to Yale," Myron continued, "he started talking to me like, all of a sudden, I'm an ignorant putz. He didn't have to borrow a penny to go there—because I was paying for it. But that's all I was good for."

Myron shook his head. "And Esther joined right in with him," he said.

Myron started rearranging some of the pieces in a showcase, moving them back and forth aimlessly.

To distract him, Hugo said, "I'm thinking of designing again."

Myron smiled at Hugo and asked, "Was it Gary's class?"

"Yes."

Myron patted Hugo on the shoulder. "I knew it!" Myron said. "I knew it would get those creative gears moving again."

"I still need a little time."

"You got it!"

"It'll be soon."

"Please, take your time," Myron said. Then he added, laughing, "Like maybe tomorrow!"

Hugo managed a soft chuckle.

On Tuesday night, a blizzard roared into Connecticut. By Wednesday morning, ten inches of snow clogged the streets and highways, with more on the way.

At ten, Hugo called Frankie.

"No dinner tonight," he said.

"My calendar is not exactly full," Frankie said. "We can reschedule."

"I can't go to work. But you work at home."

"That's right."

Because she was just a voice on the phone, Hugo felt more relaxed talking to her.

"What're you working on?" he asked.

"Are you really interested? Or are you just trying to get on my good side?"

"Both."

Frankie laughed. "Actually, I've got an impossible job to do."

"Impossible?"

"There's a big insurance company in Hartford," she said, "that just put its employees through hell. Last winter they said they had to cut expenses. So three hundred people were going to get pink slips. But that's all they said. Month after month, everybody was waiting for the axe to fall. Morale tanked. Everybody was nervous. And angry. Finally, in July..."

"July?"

"Can you believe they waited that long?"

"Terrible."

"The axe fell," Frankie said. "But after the three hundred were gone, the survivors still felt angry and bitter."

"Sure."

"So I'm writing a weekly letter from the Chairman—it goes online—explaining what happened, why they did it that way, and how happy everybody should be, now that the good times are rolling."

"Ugh!"

"If it was up to the Chairman," Frankie said, "there wouldn't be any letters."

"Why not?"

"He's a mean bastard. But he goes to church every morning. Every morning! So I guess he confesses, says a bunch of Hail Marys and then he can go back to being a bastard."

Hugo groaned.

"Human Resources wants the letters," Frankie said. "The Chairman could care less."

"You're making him look good?"

"I'm doing the best I can," she said, "but I don't think I'm fooling anybody. Hey, it's a living."

Hugo was sitting in the studio, drinking coffee and looking out at the snow storm. Frankie's voice made him feel comfortable and warm.

"When I was a kid," Frankie said, "we went to church most Sundays. But religion wasn't important to us. It was more a social thing. We didn't sit around talking about salvation. I never worried about Heaven and Hell."

"Still go to church?"

"No. I haven't for a while."

"Still not worried about Hell?" Hugo asked.

"Not worried at all. At the end, Mom said, 'When I die, the pain will be gone. That's Heaven enough.'"

"Amen."

"What about you?"

"Born Jewish," Hugo said. "Don't practice it."

"Were your parents religious?"

"No. *My* mother said, 'God didn't make this lousy world. We did.'"

"Your father?"

"He painted churches, synagogues, mosques," Hugo said. "Empty, abandoned, decaying. Signs in front saying 'Condemned' or 'For Sale'."

"That must have made him a popular guy!"

"Yeah."

Hugo was surprised at how easily he had told Frankie about this. And he didn't regret telling her.

"What are *you* doing today?" she asked.

"I don't know. Listen to music. Maybe sketch."

"Well, *some* of us have to get back to work. Why don't you call me when the streets are clear. I owe you a dinner."

"Looking forward to it."

"I am, too."

The blizzard ended on Wednesday evening. By noon on Thursday, the streets were plowed.

When Hugo called Frankie, she said, "I'd like to get together on Saturday night, if that's okay with you."

"Same time?"

"Give me an extra hour. Six o'clock."

"See you then."

Friday morning at the store, Myron greeted Hugo with a smile. "You're going to help us celebrate tonight."

"Celebrate what?"

"Vivian's getting married!"

"To the Turks and Caicos guy?"

"Yeah," Myron said. "The one who'd rather die than get married."

"You meet him yet?"

"No. He's coming to dinner tonight. We want you to be there."

"Me?"

"You know we don't have a big family," Myron said. "Esther's sister and her kids live in Cincinnati. Geoffrey is back in Washington (thank God!). You're all we've got."

"In that case..."

When he arrived at Myron's house, Vivian was there, but the Turks and Caicos guy wasn't.

"He's going to be late," Vivian explained. "Not too late, I hope. He's closing a humongous deal."

"He's a mover and shaker," Esther said, enunciating every syllable as if she were describing a world leader.

"Congratulations," Hugo said and kissed Vivian on the cheek.

They settled into the living room and Myron poured wine for everyone.

"I'm as surprised as you are," Vivian said.

"Are you happy?" Hugo asked.

"Very."

"He has an apartment," Esther gushed, "a *huge* apartment in Manhattan, on the East Side. And a beautiful summer place in Southampton."

"How do you know it's beautiful?" Vivian wondered.

"Of course it is," Esther insisted.

Vivian smiled.

"Tell me about him," Hugo said.

Vivian thought for a moment.

"His name is Arthur," she said. "Arthur Berenson."

"Artie?" Myron asked.

"No. He doesn't like 'Artie.' Call him Arthur."

"Whatever," Myron said.

"He is definitely not my Dream Husband," Vivian said.

"He's not?" (That was a disbelieving Esther.)

"He's bald," Vivian said. "I prefer men with hair."

"A minor thing," Myron said.

"He has a mustache," Vivian continued. "I don't like mustaches. Kissing is complicated."

Hugo smiled.

"He may be a little taller than me," Vivian said, "but he's short. I like tall men."

"But..." Hugo interrupted.

"But when we're together, he makes me feel wonderful," Vivian said. "Not just when we're being romantic. Whatever we do. When we sit by the pool and talk. When we take a walk on the beach. When we laugh. When we argue."

She looked at Hugo and said, "I sound like a corny movie, but I'm not being logical about it. I just want to enjoy it."

"Sure you do," he agreed.

"I suppose you can try to figure out *why* you fall in love," Vivian said. "But the only thing that matters is—you *are* in love."

The doorbell rang. Arthur had arrived.

He was bald and short. He had a bushy mustache. And Vivian showed him off proudly.

Saturday was unseasonably warm, a January day that felt as mild as October. The mounds of plowed snow all over town began to melt, leaving the streets slushy and wet.

Hugo arrived at Frankie's apartment with a gift-wrapped bottle of Cabernet in his hand, and a gift-wrapped box of earrings in the pocket of his brown corduroy jacket.

"Red wine okay?" he asked.

"Perfect," Frankie said. "We're having prime rib."

He handed her the bottle and kissed her on the cheek.

"How do you like your ribs?" she asked. "Rare? Medium? Well done?"

"Medium."

She was wearing black slacks and a white sweater. A silver-and-turquoise Native American necklace. No earrings.

"I'll open the wine," Frankie said. "There's cheese and crackers on the coffee table. Make yourself comfortable. Be back in a minute."

This time, she sat closer to him on the sofa and when he said "Cheers" she smiled and clinked her glass on his with a confident "Cheers" of her own.

"Finish the Chairman's letter?"

She nodded. "It was heart-warming."

"Does he change what you write?"

"Usually, no" Frankie said. "But one time he took out the word 'care'. I had written 'I *care* about the future of our employees.' He changed it to 'I'm *concerned* about the future of our employees.' If I were being honest, I would have written 'I don't give a shit about our employees!'"

Hugo laughed at her truthful outburst and pursued a lighter subject.

"Now tell me what you *really* think about this crazy weather."

"Snow one day, Spring the next," she rolled her eyes.

"Global warming?"

"Could be," Frankie said. "The ice caps are melting, aren't they? But New England weather has always been strange."

"True."

Frankie spread a chunk of brie on a cracker and sampled it. Hugo followed suit.

"So, you said you were going to start designing jewelry again," she said. "Or were you just thinking about it?"

"I've started."

"How does that work? You draw a design and then you make it? Or is there a company that makes it for you?"

"Usually you send it to a shop," Hugo said. "Ours is in Manhattan."

"So they produce it?"

"Yes. But sometimes the designer does. A custom-made piece."

"You can charge more, I guess," Frankie said.

"Right."

"And you've started designing again?"

"One piece so far."

"Who's producing it?"

"It's a custom piece. A gift."

"A gift? How nice," Frankie said. A timer in the kitchen began to beep-beep-beep.

Putting her wine glass down, she uttered a hurried "Sorry. Really want to hear more, but the pre-heated oven calls. Forgive me?"

"No problem," Hugo said.

He drank some wine, ate a couple of crackers and replayed again what Vivian had said: that it doesn't matter *why* you fall in love. "The only thing that matters is—you *are* in love."

Every few minutes, Frankie ran in from the kitchen, sipped some wine, said, "Be patient," or "We're getting there," and ran back. Finally, she announced a relieved, "Ta-da! It's ready."

The living room opened onto a dining area where Frankie served the prime rib, baked potatoes and green beans ("*haricots verts* with toasted, slivered almonds," she said).

"Delicious," Hugo said.

"Thank you. It *is* pretty good."

"Better than that."

They ate quietly for a few minutes.

Then Frankie said, "Now, tell me more about this 'gift' you designed."

"Later," he said.

"Why so mysterious?"

"I'll tell you later."

"Do I have to wait?"

Hugo didn't really want to wait, either.

"No," he said.

He paused and took a deep breath.

"I made something for *you,*" he said.

"For me?"

Hugo nodded and said, "To tell you..."

He couldn't finish the sentence.

Instead, he reached for the box in his jacket pocket and held it out to her. Blushing slightly, she carefully unwrapped it. But when she saw the earrings, her mood changed. Tears welled up in her eyes.

"What's wrong?" Hugo asked.

"It's not your fault," Frankie said. "You didn't know."

"Know what?"

Frankie wiped the tears away.

She began wistfully, "My ex-husband was a sort of Don Juan. Very charming. I thought he was a real prize. After my mother died, I was desperate to enjoy life again. And Phil was all about pleasure."

She held the box closer to her and studied the earrings.

"About six months after we were married," she said, "he gave me a beautiful pair of earrings. A token of his love, I thought. I wore them proudly."

She put the box down on the table.

"Later, maybe a year or so later, he gave me another pair of earrings. How wonderful, I thought."

Her eyes narrowed and her mouth tensed with anger.

"Months later, I got a call. From a woman who told me I shouldn't be so selfish. Phil loved *her*, she said. He wanted out, but he didn't want to hurt me. She really said that. It was like a bad scene from a soap opera. And that night, Phil came home with another goddamn pair of earrings."

"Guilt," Hugo said.

"Long story short, that was the end of us," Frankie said with a bitter smile. "And the end of earrings, too."

"I'll take them back."

"No. They're beautiful. I'm going to put them on."

She left the dining room for a few minutes and returned wearing the earrings.

"You designed these for me?" she asked.

"Yes," Hugo said. "To match your face. Your...style."

"Do you like the way they look?"

"Beautiful," Hugo said.

"Me? Or the earrings?"

"You."

Frankie sat down at the table.

"When I was young," she said, "it was hard for me to talk about my feelings. That's why I started writing stories. I didn't want to be Olivia, locked up inside myself. Losing everything."

Frankie reached out and took Hugo's hand.

"I don't want *you* to be Olivia, either," she said. "Tell me why you made these earrings for me."

Hugo felt his heart beat faster, a familiar dryness in his mouth.

"Tell me," Frankie gently urged. "Why did you make these beautiful earrings for me?"

"Because," he slowly relented, "I think... I'm falling in love with you."

She smiled that lovely smile. “And I’m fond of you, Hugo, so fond. But so afraid of being hurt again. Do you think we could...”

Hugo raised her hand to his lips and kissed it.

“I hope...with time,” he said.

“One thing I *can* promise,” Frankie said. “I’ll never hide my feelings from you. Can you make the same promise?”

“Yes, I can,” Hugo said tenderly, and kissed her hand again.

Empathy

Was it only a year ago? It could be a *thousand*.

I had worked late that night on a speech for my boss, the CEO.

Speechwriting takes more than talent. You have to bottle up your own identity. It's as if you become someone else—seeing the world through his eyes—and describing it in what sounds like his words—even to *him*.

The secret is *empathy*. (God, how I hate that word.)

By the time I left work that night, I was feeling pretty good. I loved my job. My girlfriend Jeanie and I were talking about getting married. Starting a family.

When I turned onto East Forty-eighth Street, I heard two or three quick explosions ahead of me, and some shouts. And then a scream. A man ran out of a restaurant halfway down the block and came toward me. He almost crashed into me, but he stopped.

He was small, shaggy-haired. His eyes were glazed with fear. And he had a gun in his right hand.

He stared at me. I thought I felt something touch me, and I was suddenly afraid. For a moment, it was as if I were in two places at once, seeing him, and seeing myself at the same time.

Abruptly, the fear in his eyes evaporated, and he smiled warmly, as if I had just given him a gift.

He raised the gun to his temple and shot himself.

A few minutes later, I told the police what I had seen. They said the young man had just killed three people, seemingly at random. No one knew who he was or why he had done it.

"Maybe he's just nuts," one policeman said. "Or spaced out on drugs."

"I guess so," I said.

A few days later, it started.

I was with Bob Hegel, the public relations vice president. Bob is a master corporate politician: calm, confident, articulate and shallow—the perfect blend for business success.

He was reading my draft of the Chairman's Letter for the Annual Report. He seemed as relaxed as ever.

But I *sensed* something else in him—a storm cloud of anger and frustration.

The cloud gathered momentum.

He was talking about the new Directors on the Board but I could somehow hear another voice, *his* voice, saying, *"The bitch is cheating on me."*

That other voice was seething with hatred: *"If I find out who it is, I'll kill the bastard. And then I'll kill her."*

Then I heard that voice whimper softly, *"I've never been able to satisfy her."*

I was frightened. I tried to clear away the angry voice, the whimper. I forced myself to hear only Bob's comments on the letter. The other voice faded.

But I began to hear more voices. In the train on the way to work. At the office. In the street.

I was listening with another set of ears that could hear what people *felt*—what they *really* felt.

"Why does he ignore me? He must know that I'm in love with him."

"He's a failure, a goddamn failure. And he won't admit it."

"Mommy, just love me, Mommy. I'm doing the best I can. Just love me."

"I wish he would die."

"I wish she would die."

"I wish I would die."

The stream of voices grew and swelled into a flood, a sea of pain.

And then I heard the other voice of my girlfriend Jeanie: *"I don't know if I want to marry him. And I sure as hell don't want a baby."*

I could hear her wondering, *"We may not be right for each other."*

I tried to hold back the tide, but I couldn't. The voices were drowning out my own thoughts, my own life.

I had to get away for a while. I told Jeanie that I was burned out, that I needed a few days by myself. I drove out to eastern Long Island, to the summer place my folks had left me. It was late September and most of the neighbors were summer people who had gone home. The voices receded. I had a chance to think about what was happening to me.

The only emotions I ever "heard" were pain, anger, fear, sadness. Never happiness or peace. It was as if I had become a safety valve, a sponge to absorb other people's misery.

That's what empathy is all about. Feeling the pain of others. But why not their happiness, too?

And *why* was I hearing those voices?

Then I realized I wasn't alone any more. I was listening with *other* ears—someone else's—or *something* else's ears. I didn't know what it was. But I knew when it had started. It was when I saw that sudden smile on the face of the man who had killed three people and then killed himself.

I *had* given him a gift. I had freed him from the voices. Because whatever it was that hears those voices had found a new home—in someone who made a living by looking at the world through other people's eyes. It had found *me*.

I knew what I had to do. I had to lower its comfort level, to put it on a starvation diet.

I left my world behind me.

I found this cottage in the woods, miles from the nearest town. Once a week, my food is delivered to me. I keep to myself. And I don't hear voices.

It wants to hear the voices. It is hungry for pain. But I don't feed it.

It is angry. But I don't care.

It wants to escape. I wish it would, but it didn't have a chance. Until today.

Two hikers lost their way in the woods. They knocked on my door. Before I opened it, I already heard his other voice—his angry voice.

"Who needs this outdoor crap? She's always got to show me how macho she is."

I opened the door.

He was a tall, handsome man, dark-haired, surly. She was slim, blonde, self-assured.

I said, "Good morning."

She said, "We're lost," but she sounded amused by the situation.

He wasn't.

He said, "We were looking for the waterfall and..."

She said, "I'm sure we're close, dear."

He nodded. "I hope so."

But I could hear him think, *"Of course I got us lost. Why should I ever do anything right? You're smarter than me. You make more money. And, as usual, I lead us right into the middle of nowhere."*

She said, "It's no big deal." Then she asked me, "Can you point us in the right direction?"

I could see the forgiveness in her eyes. The empathy.

I said, "I'll do better than that. I'll take you to a spot with the best view of the waterfall. It isn't far."

"That's very nice of you," she said.

He thought, *"Damn him. Damn her. Damn all of us."*

I led them along the steep trail to the top of the hill behind my house.

She was trying to soothe his feelings. He pretended to respond, but he was boiling with anger.

He thought, *"I wish I could throw her off this goddamn hill."*

I was calm. Even the ugliness of his thoughts didn't disturb me. It wouldn't be long now.

We reached the summit, a flat shelf of rock about thirty feet wide. I pointed to the waterfall that surged out of a nearby cliff fifty yards away.

She said, "Beautiful."

He said, "Yes. Beautiful."

He thought, *"I wish I could throw you off this goddamn hill."*

He was standing on my left; she was on my right.

I said to him, "The water is very, very cold."

He turned to look at me.

He thought, *"Idiot. Of course, it's cold."*

I pushed him off the ledge. He fell, screaming, until he hit the rocks below.

She stepped back from the edge, her eyes fearful, her mouth half open, not willing to believe what she had just seen.

I smiled at her and jumped.

The sheriff said, "He smiled at you before he jumped?"

I said, "That's right. He didn't seem to be afraid of dying."

"I'm going to type up your statement now, Miss, and then you can sign it. It'll only take a few minutes. Do you want some coffee?"

"No, thank you. I'm still shaking. I think I'll just sit here while you do it."

"Okay, Miss."

I tried to erase the terrible images from my memory but, of course, that was impossible.

I looked around the sheriff's office, at the wanted posters on the bulletin board, at the huge clock on the wall, at the tree just outside the window.

I watched the sheriff type my statement.

His hands were almost too big for the computer keyboard. He typed slowly, almost casually. He was in no hurry.

The sheriff seems to be a very self-confident man.

But he isn't. He's bitter and angry.

He doesn't show it but, somehow, I know.

Wildwood

I didn't set out to find Wildwood. We met seemingly by chance on a crisp October afternoon.

A few months earlier, I had escaped from the city to a secret cottage in the hills, where I could walk alone and breathe good air. Squirrels and sparrows and raccoons watched me suspiciously, but I never gave them cause for alarm.

My days were serendipitous. I didn't have to make plans. Or meet expectations. Or taste pleasures that always lost their flavor.

On that October afternoon, the woods spoke to me of life and death: the leaves were blazing crimson and gold. Many had fallen to earth. But the breeze still smelled faintly of Spring.

The trail I was following led me deeper and deeper into a forest thick with towering spruces and cedars. The dense canopy of leaves transformed temperate day into chilly dusk. Among the living trees, dead tree trunks were scattered, some still standing, some uprooted. I could hear an unseen woodpecker rattling nearby, harvesting his meal.

Soon, in the shady grasp of that gloomy, centuries-old forest, I could no longer feel the gentle caress of a youthful Spring breeze. I shivered with the change and, as I did, the trail disappeared in the depths of the woods.

Should I turn back?

My city answer would have been *Yes*. But I had abandoned the city and my need for certainty.

Undaunted, I continued to walk in what might or might not have been the right direction.

Abandon hope all ye who enter here.

"Good afternoon, young man."

A woman's voice, pleasant, welcoming.

She was striding boldly through the forest as if the trees and the underbrush were illusions. A Victorian novelist would have called her a "handsome woman." Tall, slender, fiftyish, her long gray hair was pulled back and tied with a colorful ribbon. She was wearing tan slacks and a bulky, dark brown sweater and seemed quite at home in the forest.

"Are you lost?" she asked.

"The trail seems to have lost *me*."

She smiled a comforting smile and said, "I can help you find it again."

"I'd appreciate that."

"May I offer you some refreshments first?" she asked.

"I don't want to trouble you."

"It's no trouble."

I followed closely behind her as she moved gracefully through the woods. It was as if the trees and bushes magically opened a path for her.

Suddenly, abruptly, the forest gave way to a broad, treeless clearing speckled with a myriad of Spring flowers still blooming in Autumn.

The woods and the lawn were sharply divided, as if a huge axe had severed the forest from the clearing. The crowds of spruces and cedars elbowed each other at the border, like hungry beggars staring through a restaurant window at dinners they will never taste.

In fact, the forest *had* been cut off from the clearing. A stone wall circled the lawn. In front of it was a deep ditch beyond which, at a lower level, the grassy clearing began.

The woman led me over a small wooden bridge that crossed the ditch.

There was a broad-shouldered two-story house in the center of the clearing, set off by its white clapboard siding and dark green shutters.

"I call my home Wildwood," the woman said.

"Though you aren't *in* the woods."

"You must never *forget* the woods," she said enigmatically.

Although I had no idea what she meant, I nodded in agreement.

I followed her into the house through a long corridor and past several closed doors. We entered a spacious sun room set in a semicircle of floor-to-ceiling windows. The room was rather bare, furnished with only four or five white wicker lawn chairs and a white wicker table. A lively floral wallpaper seemed to echo the blossoms on the lawn.

Through the windows I could see a sinuous path of stepping-stones leading to a little pond whose quiet surface mirrored the sun.

The woman sat down and invited me to sit across the table from her.

"My name is Miranda," she said.

"Prospero's daughter?"

She smiled.

"I'm David."

On the table was an open bottle of a French rosé, two long-stemmed glasses, and a platter of cheese and strawberries.

Was she expecting me? I wondered.

Miranda filled the glasses and offered me one.

"To my savior in the woods," I toasted.

"To the wild woods I saved you from," she said, touching my glass with hers.

I helped myself to a plump, succulent strawberry.

"Where were you headed today?" she asked.

"Nowhere in particular. Just enjoying the clean air. And the silence."

"Do you live nearby?"

I nodded. "Walking, maybe an hour or so from here. But I've never walked in this direction before."

Miranda studied me for a minute or two.

"You're from New York City," she said, with a knowing smile.

"Good guess."

"I can feel the tension."

I laughed. "I've been trying to slow myself down."

"You're still young, David," Miranda said. "Too soon for slowing down, isn't it?"

I looked out at the rainbow of flowers, the shimmering pond, the forest in the distance. The only thing missing was a white swan.

"Maybe so," I said. "But I wasn't ready for what happened to me. I got caught by surprise."

"Nothing serious, I hope."

"No, it just sort of happened. It wasn't planned."

"*What* happened?" she asked, her interest piqued.

"Well, right out of college I got a good job as a writer at a P.R. agency. I was there for almost five years. Lived as cheaply as I could."

"Because?"

"I was hoping to take a year or so off. I was working on a novel. Every spare minute."

"Have you found a publisher yet?"

"I haven't finished the book. Didn't even get half-way through."

She waited for me to continue. I wasn't sure I wanted to.

We sat quietly for several minutes.

Miranda refilled our glasses. The first glass had soothed me. The second made the wallpaper flowers more vivid, more real. Then they became more surreal.

"I was at a party," I said. "Ran into a guy I knew in college. I hadn't seen him since then. He's a commercial artist. Website design. When I told him I was a writer, he smiled encouragingly and asked me what *kind* of writer. 'An unpublished one,' I said."

Miranda nodded and shifted impatiently, as if she were hearing my story for the *second* time.

"'I'm in need of a writer', he said, and he really meant it. He wanted to collaborate on a graphic novel. He was sure we could make a ton of money if we pushed the right buttons."

"And he knew which buttons to push?"

"He got me thinking about the possibilities."

I paused.

"The possibilities," she said, softly.

"I started with a couple of assumptions. First, most people nowadays have short attention spans. They don't want to spend time thinking. Second, they love to feed off social media. Third, they love gimmicks, twists. O'Henry would be making it big today."

"But, David, weren't you working on a novel?" she asked.

"I was frustrated. Tired of digging deep. Revising. I began to doubt I would ever write the final page."

Miranda sighed.

"I haven't abandoned my novel. I just had to set it aside. Temporarily."

"And now you're the new O'Henry?"

I ignored the reproach in her voice. "You could say that."

She watched me as I reached for another strawberry and finished my wine. She picked up the bottle and leaned forward to refill my glass.

"No more, thank you," I said.

She replaced the bottle on the tray.

"I came up with what I called *splashes*—quirky short-short stories," I said. "A couple of hundred words wrapped around quirky graphics. Working as well online as in print. Not really a new form. But it had a new name—and it caught on. Who knows why? Went viral, as they say."

"And so much easier to write than a novel."

"It still takes talent," I said, defensively. "I can show you. If you go online..."

"I don't have a computer," Miranda said.

"Use your cell phone."

"I don't have a cell phone. Or any phone."

"So you're a Luddite?" I said.

"Technology has no heart."

I raised my wine glass. "I guess I'd better have a refill, after all."

Miranda poured the wine and waited while I drank thoughtfully.

"Well, maybe I can't *show* you," I said. "But all is not lost. On our publicity tours, there was one story I would *perform*. There were images flashing on a screen behind me. I know it by heart. I think I deliver it pretty well."

She sat up straight and folded her hands in her lap expectantly but not cheerfully, like a child anticipating punishment.

"It's called 'Vermin'," I said.

The planet was never too warm or too cold.

The water, as crystal clear as fine glass, flowed through rolling, blue-green hills.

Tiny, shimmering leaves in silver trees rang like gentle bells in the soft, soothing breezes.

Stately, elegant cities rose from the plains. The walls of the towering, graceful buildings were ablaze with exquisite abstract murals. The city squares were filled with massive, mysterious stone shapes.

And with tall bronze, almost-human creatures—we called them Angels—who learned our language in an hour, spent their days laughing, making music, making love, drinking sweet wine brewed from the honey of giant, stingless bees. The Angels never made war or killed an animal or plant: their bodies turned sun- and star-light into food.

I called the planet Paradise, and no one in my crew disagreed.

They welcomed us, those bronzed Angels, with a serenity that was almost indifference. They seemed to feel no fear and, despite the evidence of their labors—their soaring, wondrously-fashioned cities, their shimmering robes, their delicate, transparent harps—we never saw them work.

But, alas, there *was* a flaw in Paradise: vermin. Hordes of hostile, repulsive little purple things with huge heads and too many eyes, too many hands and legs, and screeching, buzzing voices. They were everywhere.

Although the Angels didn't pay much attention to these creatures, we knew that Paradise would be far more beautiful without them. But the Angels had never learned to kill.

We carefully analyzed the planet's unique ecological balance, so we knew that, on Paradise, every life form was self-sufficient. No Darwinian struggle for survival.

We did the killing for the Angels.

Goodbye, vermin.

When it was over, as my crew began to clear away the remains, I sat by a crystal stream and asked one of the Angels a question I had postponed for much too long: "How did you build your cities?"

"We didn't," he said.

Pointing at one of the purple carcasses, he added, "*They* did."

"That was a nice performance, David," Miranda said.

"I guess I'm a ham at heart."

I sat back in my chair. I waited for her to say more, but she didn't.

"The images add a lot to the stories," I said.

"Quirky images," she said, as if to reassure me that she was listening to what I had told her.

"Right. Well, as I said, the 'splashes' really clicked. We became—not famous, but *almost* famous."

Miranda laughed.

"I mean, if you were into graphic novels, you knew who we were."

"I'll take your word for it."

"Do you watch late-night TV?" I asked.

She shook her head.

"No TV set," I guessed.

"No TV set."

"If you had one, you might have seen us on the late-night shows. We made the rounds."

"Did you enjoy that?" she asked.

"Not really," I said. "The programs are taped much earlier in the day. So it isn't really late at night. And it's not as relaxed as it looks. If they screw up something, they redo it. The set looks pretty good on TV but it's cheesy-looking when you see it up close."

"It doesn't sound as if I'm missing much," Miranda said.

"But it was great publicity for us. We started to make money."

"Quirky money?" she asked, smiling at her own joke.

"*Real* money," I said.

"What did you spend it on?"

"Everything that's first class," I said. "Food, wine. Travel. New friends. The good life."

"Why didn't that make you happy?" she asked.

"I *am* happy."

"Is that why you're hiding in the woods?"

I felt a flash of anger, not at her but at myself.

"I'm not hiding!"

Miranda shook her head. "What *are* you doing?"

"I'm taking a break," I said, too softly to be convincing.

And Miranda *wasn't* convinced.

"You're taking a break from being happy?" she wondered.

I pretended that was a rhetorical question.

"My mother and father are proud of me," I said. "I've made *them* almost famous, too. Well, maybe not, but they can finally brag about me."

After a polite pause she asked "Why aren't you still living the *good life*?"

Although she was challenging me, Miranda's voice was gentle, her expression, sympathetic.

"Some people were disappointed in me," I said. "My sister, Liz, gave me a hard time."

"Why?"

"She's three years younger than me. Smart kid. Talented. She's up in Maine, working for peanuts at a regional theater. Wants to direct plays."

"Why was she disappointed?"

"She says I always encouraged her to follow her dreams. That's what kept her going. And now I've let her down, she says, by not following *mine*. By wasting my talent."

"What did you tell her?"

"To be patient with me."

Miranda knew I had more to say. She waited.

"The woman I was living with left me," I said.

"She didn't want to live the 'good life' with you?"

"She thought it was the *bad* life."

Miranda studied me for a moment, then said, "You thought she may be right?"

"Yes," I said. "And I was beginning to worry about surviving. I could feel the merry-go-round going faster and faster. The world became a blur. I had to jump off."

I had run out of words. Miranda let the silence wrap itself around us like a friendly embrace.

The sun-dappled pond, the flowery lawn and the dark forest looked like a colorful landscape painted on the tall windows of the sun room. I wished I could absorb the serenity of that scene. But all I felt was weariness.

I don't know how much time passed before Miranda said, "When I met you today, you were lost in the woods. Later, when I asked you where you were headed, you said, 'nowhere in particular.' Isn't that the same as being lost?"

"Maybe."

"You keep talking about life *happening* to you," she said, "as if you're not making choices. It seems as if the only choice you *could* make was to run away."

"That's not fair."

"Of course you can't control everything," Miranda said. "No one can. But choosing to go nowhere is not a choice. It's an excuse."

"What do you want me to do?" I asked.

Miranda smiled and said, "It isn't up to me, David. What do *you* want to do?"

"I'm not sure I know."

"I think you do."

When I didn't respond, Miranda said, "I told you that I call this house Wildwood, even though it's not in the woods. Because no matter how far we are from the forest, we are never really safe. There are always wild things stalking us. And we have to accept that and embrace it. There's no easy way out of the woods. If there isn't a path, you have to fight your way through."

"What if you can't get through?" I asked.

"There's only one way to find out."

I looked out at the peaceful lawn and the glowing pond, then beyond them at the dense, shadowy woods.

I stood up. The after-effects of the wine seemed to vanish almost instantly.

"Will you show me the way back?" I asked.

Miranda also stood up but she said, "I don't have to. You'll find it."

I'm not sure how, but I did.

In a few days, I returned to the City.

I gradually eased myself out of the good life. First, I wrote a new set of splashes. With the money I earned, plus the sale price of my condo, I could comfortably settle down to writing my novel again.

But of course, it wasn't the same story. It was better. Less aggressive. It took me more than a year and a half to complete the first draft. During that time, I kept mostly to myself. And I discovered that I could resist everything, *including* temptation.

My book disappointed my parents and upset my fans, who deserted me *en masse*.

My sister was delighted. I tried to win back my former lover, but she didn't trust me any more, and I didn't blame her.

My publisher was surprised when I finally delivered my manuscript. The book became a best seller because my name was on it. But it disappointed anyone who expected a 350-page splash. Only two or three reviewers favored the novel. Most weren't enthusiastic. But I did attract a new, much smaller audience.

I was pleased with the book. It's far from a masterpiece but I thought it was a good start.

I wanted Miranda to read it, but you can't call or text someone who doesn't own a telephone. Or email someone who doesn't have a computer.

I tried to find Wildwood again, but I couldn't. Not when I tried to retrace my steps in the woods. Not in a search of the county records.

"Miranda" is the feminine form of a Latin word that means "strange" or "wonderful". It can even be stretched to mean "miraculous".

But I'm not a religious man. I don't believe in miracles.

Fair Play

Innocence can be appealing. Especially when it comes wrapped in smooth young skin and sleek, tender muscle. And when you look into those hungry, nineteen-year-old eyes, you can't help remembering your own first woman-to-woman pleasure.

But now, although you're just a few years older than your student, *you're* the experienced one, the teacher.

Yes, innocence can be appealing. But, sad to say, it's a mixed bag. I don't always want to be the seducer. And with Laurel, who never seemed to take the lead, no matter how much I taught her, I began to get downright resentful.

I didn't keep that a secret.

With a cold, matter-of-fact appraisal, I dismissed her: "I'm sorry, sweetheart, but it's just not working for me anymore."

She was curled up on my bed, naked. A thin film of sweat reflected the sunlight streaming through the window.

She was still feeling the hot waves of pleasure. She was content. I wasn't.

She tried to concentrate on what I was saying, but she was distracted by the aftershocks she felt.

Reluctantly, she sat up and asked, "What isn't working?"

"You and me, babe."

"But I love you. Don't you know that?"

"You don't love me, Laurel. You love *it*."

"How can you say that?"

Her eyes filled with tears.

"I can say that because I've been there," I said. "When I was eighteen, she was thirty. I thought I would love her till the day I died. She didn't plan to hang around that long."

"You sound so cruel."

She wiped away tears with her fingertips. She looked so cute that I almost caved. But I didn't.

"It's time to say goodbye, sweetheart," I said. "I'm sorry, but believe me, this is the right thing for both of us."

She didn't believe me. I learned that the hard way.

For a few weeks, I was in limbo. I have to admit it: I missed Laurel. At the same time, I felt freer, more relaxed, and determined not to go down the same I'll-be-the-teacher path again. Not for a while anyway.

In short, I was on the prowl for a stronger, wiser woman, one who would take charge. I wanted to fall asleep with my head resting on her soft breasts. I wanted to feel her sheltering arms embrace me. I wanted to be the young one.

I thought I had found her one night at the *Pas de deux*, a club on the Upper East Side. I'm not a regular there. It caters to an older crowd but, considering what I was looking for, it seemed like the right place to start.

I had a couple of beers at the bar, a couple of conversations, but didn't feel any good vibes. I was about to leave when she sat down next to me.

She was in her early forties, tall, lean and long-legged. Her hair was dark brown, threaded with natural gray highlights. Her eyes were deep and dark, her cheekbones beautifully shaped. She had the look of a woman who could run a company or a country—and, more important, take me to Paradise and back.

"My name is Eleanor," she said. "You look like you need a friend."

"I'm Katherine, and I need more than that."

She smiled seductively, put her arm around my shoulder and said, "That sounds promising."

Eleanor always seemed to find a new way to arouse me, to tempt me, to satisfy me. And when she wasn't stimulating my body, she was stimulating my mind. She was intelligent, witty.

When I wasn't with her, I was unhappy. When I *was* with her, I dreaded the moment when she would say, "I'll see you tomorrow," and go home.

One night in my apartment after we made love, I asked her, "Why don't we live together?"

"No," she said. "I enjoy my freedom."

"I understand. But for the first time in my life, I'm really in love. I love you, Eleanor. I never thought I'd say this, but I don't think I can live without you."

"I think you can," she said. "In fact, I'm sorry to say it's just not working for me anymore."

"What isn't working?" I asked, a question that sounded familiar to me.

"You and me, babe."

Another echo of the past.

"I don't understand," I said.

"It isn't complicated. I'm tired of our relationship. It doesn't satisfy me."

"I can change. I'll do whatever you want me to do."

She smiled, but her eyes were cold and angry.

"I want you to think about me," she said, "remember me, and know that I'll never make love to you again."

"Why are you doing this?"

She walked to the door, opened it, smiled again and said, "I'm Laurel's mother."

Second Sight

listen: there's a hell
of a good universe next door; let's go
—e.e. cummings

One of the dreariest places in the civilized world is an airline terminal during a snowstorm. Hordes of indignant would-be passengers wander the waiting rooms and corridors, choleric nomads, glaring at ticket agents and cursing the Wright Brothers.

For almost twenty years, Steven Fowler had commuted on the Long Island Railroad from Huntington to his office in Manhattan, so he could endure travel delays with practiced equanimity. Now, on his way home from a corporate meeting in Chicago, he was stranded at O'Hare Airport, calmly sitting in a bar, watching wind-driven sheets of snow through a tall picture window, and drinking Martinis ever so slowly.

Someone three stools away claimed that the weather forecast on his iPad promised a break in the storm "soon."

"And on Friday, an end to world hunger," Steven stage-whispered.

The drinker next to him laughed and said, "I'm from warm, cozy Baltimore. What the hell am I doing in Chicago?"

"I had to be here on business," Steven said. "You, too?"

The man shook his head.

"No. My daughter lives here. Married a guy she met at the University of Chicago. I think he's a schmuck, but she says he's a genius."

"He could be both," Steven suggested.

"I figured I'd play it safe. Wait till April to visit her. Did me a lot of good."

He extended his hand. "Sammy Bloomberg."

Steven shook his hand. "Steven Fowler."

Sammy Bloomberg was not someone you'd look at twice. He was a short, round-shouldered man in his late forties. He wore a terrible hair-piece. His face was bland, his eyes shielded by heavy lenses. Steven thought Sammy could probably commit murder on a crowded street and get away with it: no one would remember seeing him.

"What business are you in?" Sammy wondered.

"Electronics. Components for computers, cell phones, printers. Company called Monitrex. I'm in Sales. You never heard of us."

Sammy sighed. "That computer shit drives me nuts," he said.

"What's *your* game?"

Sammy smiled. "My *game*? I own a shoe store. Shoes, I understand."

"I'll bet you use computers for billing," Steven said. "And for keeping track of your inventory."

"Yeah. A young guy who works for me does all of that."

"These days, you've got no choice."

Sammy nodded in agreement and ordered another beer. He took the last cashew nut from a nearby bowl and asked the bartender for more.

"We could be here forever," he said.

"It'll just *seem* like forever."

The wind kicked up outside, adding its icy voice to the conversation.

Sammy sampled the newly-arrived cashews, drank some beer from his refilled glass and said, "Every time I'm on a plane I think, *How in God's name can this fucking thing fly?* It's a big, gigantic fucking load of steel. Tons of it. With 200 people on it. And a million pieces of luggage. And you're telling me the fucking air is holding it up?"

"You can't argue with success," Steven observed.

"You understand how it works?"

"Not really."

"But you're not worried?"

"You ever heard of William James?" Steven asked.

"He was a writer, wasn't he?"

"That was *Henry* James. His brother William was a philosopher."

"My son-in-law teaches philosophy. I don't think he knows how to change a light bulb."

Steven laughed. "William wasn't like that. He was a practical guy. Someone once asked him if he believed in baptism. He said, 'Believe in it? I've seen it.'"

Sammy thought for a moment, smiled and said, "Yeah, okay. I think I get it."

"Airplanes *do* fly, so I don't worry about what keeps them up."

Sammy nodded, but he didn't look convinced.

Steven ate a handful of cashews and watched the wind change the path of the snow from vertical to horizontal.

Sammy asked, "You always dreamed of being a salesman? I mean when you were a kid."

Steven shook his head and said, "No. I kind of fell into it."

"What *did* you want to be, when you were a kid? A doctor? A lawyer?"

"My mother is a doctor. A pediatrician. She's still practicing. My father is a dentist."

Sammy was impressed. "Where did you live? Park Avenue?"

"Brooklyn Heights. A nice neighborhood."

"I'll bet. So how come you didn't become a doctor?"

"It didn't interest me," Steven said. "And I wouldn't be a dentist for anything in the world. You know, a lot of them commit suicide."

"No shit?"

"Do you blame them? Spending your whole life with terrified people drooling all over you."

"And your folks didn't push you?"

"They were too busy working," Steven said. "And my father was into politics, too. He was elected head of the county dental association two or three times. My mother did volunteer work a couple of days a week for kids from poor families. I guess they didn't have much time to worry about *me*."

"So you became a salesman."

"A friend of my father's who was a vice president at Monitrex got me a job in Sales. I'm pretty good at schmoozing with people. I can tell a joke. I was doing okay, if not setting the world on fire."

Steven grabbed a handful of cashews and ordered another Martini.

"Then the company had a golf outing," Steven continued. "I have a three handicap."

"Is that good?"

"Very good. The vice president of Sales, my father's friend, was running the event. He was in the CEO's foursome and he put me in it, too. He knew how well I play."

"So you impressed the boss?"

"I did. But of course I let him beat me."

"Sure."

"Not by much," Steven said. "A couple of years later, when the vice president was kicked upstairs, I took his place. I was only twenty-nine. Like I said, it just happened."

"I didn't have any dreams, either," Sammy said. "I didn't care what I did, as long as I made money. I figured the best thing would be to have my own business. A hardware store, maybe. I always liked walking around hardware stores looking at the tools and all the other crap."

"But you didn't end up in the hardware business?"

"It didn't turn out that way. I had my eye on a shoe store downtown. The owner was this old guy. He hadn't fixed it up in a long time and it looked like shit. But it was in a good spot. Lots of traffic," Sammy grinned shrewdly. "I was working in a furniture store at the time, making big commissions. I was single and living at home. My father had passed away, leaving the house to Mom with the mortgage paid off. So I was able to save a bundle."

"You bought the shoe store."

"Fixed it up," Sammy said. "Carried only top-line brands. Did well. Still doing well. I may buy another store."

"So I guess we're both practical people. We made it without dreams."

They watched the storm cover the world with a pale blanket.

"It was my daughter who got me thinking about dreaming," Sammy said. "She asked me to tell her husband—the philosopher, the schmuck—about my brother Seth. About something that happened a long time ago."

"Does he know your brother?"

Sammy shook his head and said, "My brother is not here anymore."

Steven was puzzled about Sammy's choice of words.

"You mean he's dead?"

"Do I?"

"Sammy, you're not talking like a practical man."

Sammy looked out at the snow. And then past the snow.

"My brother was a dreamer," he said. "He was smart. Smarter than most people. He read a lot. Teachers loved him."

"Was he younger?" Steven asked. "Older?"

"Three years older. A tough act to follow. But he was a good guy. I didn't mind."

"And he was a dreamer?"

"Yeah. He read poetry. He was going to *be* a poet. He would teach in college and write poetry. That was his dream."

"Sounds kind of practical to me," Steven said.

"He got a scholarship to Cornell."

"So maybe dreams can come true."

"Not really," Sammy said. "At first, he did okay. Better than okay. One professor there—a big shot—really liked his poems. Encouraged him. Seth met a girl, too, also into poetry. She had the same prof."

"Sounds good."

"He was happy. And it wasn't just his writing. He was crazy about this girl. He said she was still a virgin. And even though everybody was doing it, she told him she wasn't ready."

"But it didn't work out?"

"His prof—this great teacher—wrote a book of poems—published it. Turns out he stole a lot of my brother's stuff. Sure, he made some changes in it. Maybe made it better. Who knows? But he stole a lot."

"Could he get away with that?"

"How do you prove it? He was Seth's teacher. He could say he was the one who really wrote the stuff."

"So he screwed your brother."

"Not just my brother. Turns out that the virgin wasn't a virgin. Thanks to the professor."

"What did your brother do?"

"I got to give him credit," Sammy said. "He didn't give up. He kept writing, kept dreaming. He graduated with high honors. Got a teaching job at Amherst."

"Great school."

"There he met another woman, a teacher at the college. They got married. She was nice enough, I guess. But when she was thirty-one she had a baby and decided to retire."

"You mean, forever?"

"That's what I mean," Sammy said. "My brother wasn't earning much. He had already published two books of poetry. Nobody liked them. I don't know why. Maybe he wasn't that good."

Steven nodded.

"His wife wanted another kid. He said they couldn't afford another kid. So she leaned on him, cried a lot, finally made him quit teaching. He got a job on a flashy, shitty men's magazine. But the pay was good. He started writing stories for the magazine. And for others, too. He was making more money. His wife was happy. They had another kid."

Steven wasn't sure he wanted to hear any more, but Sammy kept going.

"Then my brother started having medical problems," Sammy said. "Well, one problem. He started to go blind."

Now Steven *knew* he didn't want to hear any more, but he also knew he couldn't interrupt Sammy.

"It was a crazy kind of blindness," Sammy said. "The doctors tested him and there was nothing wrong with his eyes—or his brain, or anything—but he was definitely going blind."

"Psychosomatic," Steven said.

"And that wasn't the worst part. He told us that, as he was losing his sight *here*, he was beginning to see another world somewhere else."

"What the hell does that mean?"

Sammy shrugged. "He told us that this other world was getting clearer and clearer. It was a better place to live, he said. It was peaceful. The people there were nicer than us."

"I don't understand."

"We didn't either. And when he couldn't see at all, he talked more and more about this *other* world."

"You said 'crazy'. You're right," Steven said.

"And then, one morning, he was gone."

"You mean, mentally?"

"No. I mean *gone*. He was in the hospital. For more tests. The nurse checked on him at three in the morning. He was sleeping. At six, he was gone."

"Your brother was blind, right?"

"Yeah."

"So he didn't walk out and catch a flight to Tahiti," Steven said.

"No one saw him leave. The security cameras didn't pick him up. He just disappeared."

"Where did he go?"

"We don't know. We never saw him again. There was a big police investigation. His wife even went on TV. Nothing. He never showed up anywhere. That was almost twenty years ago."

The dreary snow-bound airport and the multiple Martinis had dulled Steven's senses, but he somehow felt threatened by Sammy's story.

"Are you snowing me?" he asked. "No pun intended."

"It's the truth," Sammy said. "The story was in the Baltimore papers for a couple of months. You can look it up."

"Where do *you* think he is?"

Sammy shrugged.

"I don't know. I don't believe in other worlds."

"I don't care if you're a dreamer or not," Steven said. "There's no such place."

"You're right."

"So whatever happened to him, he didn't go off to some La-La-Land."

"Okay," Sammy said.

"Okay," Steven said.

They sat silently for the next hour or so, watching the storm.

The iPad prediction turned out to be true. The storm blew by, but it was another five hours before Steven's flight took off. Sammy's left a little earlier.

They said a quick, uncomfortable *Goodbye*.

Back home, Steven's job as V.P. Sales was a trifle monotonous, but lucrative. His marriage to the girl next door was serene, but unexciting. His son and daughter were moderately successful, but unremarkable.

He kept the story of Sammy's brother at the fringes of his memory. It was just a tall story. Very tall.

But now and then, when he was alone, he would look up and search the sky, wondering if he might catch a glimpse of something—a world that only dreamers see.

Tiny Town

The last time I saw Tiny Town, I was a teenager. That was more than twenty years ago. It was shabby then. Now, on a frozen November night, it seemed to be virtually abandoned.

Tiny Town wasn't really a town. It was a neighborhood—a few narrow streets, like a twisted tick-tack-toe grid—on the edge of the village of Hanford, Connecticut, where I grew up.

"Years ago, before you were born, that whole section south of the lake was slated to be a summer resort," my Dad told me. "They even had a name for it: Hanford Waterside. A developer built some bungalows, but then most of the land by the lake was sold to the lumber mill."

The lumber company also bought hundreds of acres of surrounding woodland, raw material for the mill.

"Thank God the big marsh separates the village from the mill—all the noise and dirt," Dad said. "But that killed Hanford Waterside."

We children called the place Tiny Town because the bungalows looked like doll houses, even up close. They were packed tightly together on small, scrubby chunks of land. And the twisted streets were barely one car wide. If a driver met a car coming the other way, one of the cars would have to back up into a driveway or a cross-street to let the other pass.

There were few trees in Tiny Town, but the mill made up for the lack of wood, shedding a fine mist of sawdust into the air that coated every roof and lawn and sidewalk.

I had childhood nightmares about Tiny Town, claustrophobic nightmares. I was forced to live in one of those seedy little houses on one of those barren, twisted streets. The rooms kept getting smaller. The walls kept closing in on me. And I knew I could never leave.

Years ago, I did leave Hanford for New Haven. But this evening after work, I made the hour-and-a-half drive back to the village where I grew up, back to Tiny Town.

I parked on one of its narrow streets. Most of the bungalows were abandoned, boarded up, shuttered. Lights burned in only a handful of them.

The last of the trees had died. I could hear the saws in the lumber mill this late in the day, still whining their endless, nasty song. An icy nor'easter screamed across the lake, scattering clouds of sawdust on Tiny Town. And on me.

I sat in my car in the darkness and thought about why I had returned to this childhood nightmare. There were so many reasons.

My father was a gentleman and he was a gentle man.

"He's got no spark," my mother said. "He's not a fighter."

She wasn't angry about that. Or disappointed. And she wasn't complaining. She would always add, "And he's the love of my life."

Dad was a lawyer, a partner in a firm with two lifelong friends, Al and Howie, who did all the heavy lifting. Al was an expert in contract law. Howie specialized in divorce cases. Dad handled only the routine stuff—wills, real estate, now and then a minor law suit. Fortunately, he rarely had to appear in court. I can vouch for the fact that he was not particularly persuasive. I saw him plead a couple of cases and he was too cautious, too hesitant. He didn't want to hurt anyone's feelings.

Al once told me why he and Howie didn't mind the uneven distribution of labor: "We've known your Dad forever, since we were kids. He's a good guy. A lot better than Howie or me. So we carry the load. So what! He helps keep us out of trouble."

Dad had wanted to study English Lit, to teach in college. His father came down hard on that idea. Grandpa had struggled to make a living, working on an assembly line in a textile mill, living paycheck-to-paycheck in a company town, a life that killed his spirit.

And then he killed Dad's spirit: "Teaching is a dead end," Grandpa warned. "You'll never make a living."

Dad didn't fight back. He went to law school at night. He didn't graduate with honors. He wasn't the editor of the Law Review. And he didn't enjoy being a lawyer. But he made Grandpa happy.

Reading was Dad's only hobby—not best sellers or detective stories. Only the great writers. He tried unsuccessfully to get my older brother, Michael, to read those books, but Michael wasn't a reader. He didn't even go to college. Instead, he became an electrician and did very well for himself.

That didn't impress Dad. I was his last hope.

I tried. Believe me, I tried. I majored in English. I worked hard at being the intellectual Dad wanted me to be. But I was out of my element. And my grades showed it.

In my junior year, I finally told him I was switching majors: "I'll get a Business degree. I'm good with people. I bet I can make it in marketing or sales."

He didn't argue with me.

A week before my graduation, he had a stroke. He lived only two more years, unable or unwilling to speak, detached from life, crippled in every sense.

When he died, I knew I had failed him, just as he had failed himself.

In the cold light of a full moon, the little houses of Tiny Town looked even smaller and lonelier. The stars seemed not only distant, but indifferent. They had burned for billions of years while my life would flare up and die too quickly for them to notice. It didn't matter to them why I came back. But it mattered to me.

On the company's org chart, Jack Lopez was the Assistant Secretary, reporting to the Vice President-Secretary/Treasurer. But that's not how he described his job.

"I'm an expediter," he would say. "*They* know I can get things done for them, so they don't have to do the dirty work."

They were the CEO, CFO and the rest of the top brass. And because of the unpleasant, unethical, sometimes illegal *things* he did for them, Jack knew he had his job for life.

About a year-and-a-half ago, on a frigid, gray winter morning, Jack called me. I had just arrived at the office and was savoring my first hot cup of coffee.

"Would you stop by and see me?" he asked. "The sooner the better."

His voice was as cold as the winter morning.

I was only a sales manager, not important enough to be one of Jack's clients.

Why does he want to see me?

I knew he wasn't going to give me a bonus. At the last department meeting a few days ago my boss, Ted Graham, the V.P. Sales, had said, "You know, Mark, your team isn't pulling its weight."

"Yeah, like I've told you, Ted, we've had shake-ups at a couple of our biggest customers. New buyers," I reminded him. "It's like starting from scratch."

"That's *your* problem. *My* problem is the bottom line."

Jack Lopez's office was all hard edges. No plants, no art work on the walls. One photograph of his wife and son. And no folders or correspondence on his desk. Just an In/Out box. And, this morning, a blue Personnel folder.

Jack was in his early fifties, a puffy, slow-moving man with a humorless smile and bleary, pale blue eyes behind thick, bifocal lenses.

"Sit down, Mark."

"What can I do for you?"

Jack pursed his lips.

"How long have you been with us, Mark?"

"Almost fourteen years. I was the second salesman hired, back when we were in that old brick warehouse in Stratford."

Jack wasn't in the company then. It was a great time. We were young and aggressive, starting out with a bare-bones operation, certain that we would make it big. We were bankrolled by the Levitt brothers, the partners who owned the company.

We did grow. We did make a name for ourselves. In eight years, we became a public company and all of the original fifteen employees were rewarded with options.

During the early years, I was riding high. But then my sweet times turned sour. A couple of major deals went south. I began to lose my touch, my confidence, my traction with customers. I didn't know why. I began to press too hard. Younger men passed me by and I never caught up with them again.

Jack Lopez didn't waste time reminiscing. He opened the blue folder and riffled through the pages, stopping to read something now and then. I sat and watched him and listened to the wind's harsh whisper.

"Your 401K is substantial," he said. "And you have a shit-load of options."

"Yes."

Jack looked up from the folder and closed it.

"We know what you've done for the company," he said.

He leaned forward with his elbows on the desk. He pressed the chubby fingers of his right hand against the fingers of his left and peered at me coyly from behind that wall.

"But in business, the past doesn't matter," Jack said. "It's what we made the last quarter that counts."

"I know."

He flexed his fingers, as if he were exercising them. Then he lowered his hands and sighed.

"Ted is worried," he said. "All of us are."

"I'm sure I can turn it around soon."

Jack smiled his empty smile.

"We can't wait," he said.

"Maybe if I..."

Jack stood up and said, "You'll get six months severance and three weeks pay for the vacation you didn't take."

"You mean I...?"

Jack nodded. "I have to stay with you while you pack your personal belongings. Then I'll escort you out."

Ted, who had hired me fourteen years ago, didn't fire me. Or say Thank You or Good Luck. He asked the "expediter" to do his dirty work.

My wife, Denise, wasn't surprised that I lost my job.

"How many times have I told you to leave?" she asked. "You used to be on the fast track. But you never took advantage of it."

"I did pretty well."

She frowned. "You should have left years ago. You're always afraid to make a move."

Denise was a brilliant forty-five-year-old, still very much in love with her job teaching English at Wesleyan University.

We were both twenty when we fell in love and got married. And we planned to take the world by storm.

She did. I didn't.

She was a lot smarter than me. But she was shy. I wasn't. I wooed her with style, impressed her with my confidence.

After a time, when her career blossomed, and my confidence crumbled, she became impatient with me, restless. She was right: I couldn't keep up with her. She found someone who could, Guy Kennedy, a professor of history at Wesleyan. I didn't blame her. Our marriage had disintegrated.

"I think Don is your best bet," Denise said. "You worked in electronics. It's the same business."

Don, her brother, owned a chain of stores that sold computers, cell phones and the like. He was successful and he had no respect for me at all.

"First, let me see what I can find on my own."

Denise shrugged.

After dinner, she said, "I'm going out."

She didn't bother to make up lies anymore. She was going to meet Guy. And she knew I didn't care.

There was a strange, comfortable inertia in our relationship. We didn't mind living together and apart at the same time. It was a kind of emotional laziness, I guess. For me, it was like having a roommate who used to be a close friend, but had drifted away. I don't know what it was like for her. We never talked about it.

Guy was separated from his wife, but Denise said they were Catholic and didn't believe in divorce.

"Divorce is a sin, but adultery isn't?" I wondered.

That night after she left, I called Margaret Braun. I could say that she was my lover, but we didn't love each other. We didn't demand love from each other.

Marge was a fashion illustrator. A very talented artist. She was only twenty-eight, but she wasn't interested in men her age. She wanted to fill in the "lover" slot on her resume without making a major emotional commitment. That was just my speed. And I didn't have to spend Saturday night by myself.

Why not *love*? Denise may have needed it. I didn't.

The saws in the lumber mill had been switched off. The lights in the bungalows were dark now. But I still sat there in the darkness, parked on one of the narrow, twisted streets of Tiny Town. It was getting colder. I turned on the engine and the heat.

And I thought of my daughter Janice.

She was our only child, as smart as her mother, bright-eyed and winsome. I was so proud of her. And when she was little, I was special to her.

But as she matured, Denise—a successful, independent woman, a brilliant scholar, a respected teacher—became her role model. And I couldn't compete for Janice's affection. Or maybe I stopped trying.

Denise decided that Janice would go to Yale (Denise's alma mater). Janice earned a scholarship and was on the Dean's List every term during her Freshman, Sophomore and Junior years. In the middle of her Senior year, she dropped out, married a penniless photographer and moved to a farm in Oregon to "live a simple life." She sent us photographs of her feeding chickens, milking a cow, breast-feeding her first-born baby, and her second-born.

I was disappointed. I felt that my daughter was wasting her talent and her life. Denise was delighted.

"I love her spirit," she said.

When Janice called us, she mostly wanted to talk to Denise. I was merely a bystander.

We went out to see her and her family a few times. Janice and Denise kissed and hugged and chattered. I tried to find something to say to Janice's husband, who always found an excuse to avoid me—working in the darkroom, setting up shoots.

He was a stranger to me. And so was my only child.

I tried desperately to find a job on my own. I couldn't. I think Jack Lopez may have put out the bad word to his contacts. Maybe not.

Anyway, I went to work for Denise's brother Don. I'm the manager of his Hamden store. The assistant manager, Phil, hates me. He thinks the only reason I got the job is because of my relationship to Don. He's right. He runs the store for me.

Actually, the store could run itself. I do the paper work and go to Don's sales meetings and we keep making money.

I get up every morning and do what I have to do. I watch my wife live her life. I go through the motions with Margaret Braun. I think of my lovely, accomplished daughter and wish she cared whether I live or die.

And tonight, I drove back to Tiny Town.

When I was a child, Tiny Town was a claustrophobic nightmare, a narrow, twisted, hopeless prison, that could crush my spirit. When I was a child, I wondered what it would be like to live in Tiny Town forever.

Now I know.

Cassie

The whirligig of time brings in his revenges.
—*Twelfth Night*, Shakespeare

Professor George Richmond couldn't believe it.

He studied the strong, Gallic face of his colleague at New York University, Professor Julie Bergerac.

"You're Cassie Carlson's daughter?" he asked.

"Cassie *Bergerac's,*" she said.

"Henri Bergerac was your father."

Julie smiled and said, "As you can see, I look like *him*, not her."

George nodded in agreement.

"I fell in love with your mother," George said. "From afar, of course. About forty years ago. I was a senior in high school."

"She was a beautiful woman. Still is."

"And she's coming here?"

"Tomorrow." Julie said."To my Classic Films class."

"Cassie," George whispered reverentially.

Julie sighed.

"Most people have forgotten her," she said.

"I haven't. I've got DVD's of all her movies."

"God bless you," Julie said, with a trace of sincerity.

There was a time long ago when Cassandra "Cassie" Carlson was Movieland's flavor of the month. But the flavor didn't last. After a brief career, Cassie had disappeared.

"Her discovery was a big story at the time," George said.

"A coed at Oklahoma State rescued from obscurity by Nelson Spector," Julie said.

She frowned and added, "He wasn't much of a director. Just a promoter. And *Maman* says he was a genuine son of a bitch."

Nelson Spector had made his reputation by challenging the Establishment. His movies were stark, sensual and perversely enigmatic.

In an article in *Cahiers du cinéma,* François Truffaut wrote that Spector "has everything Antonioni has except talent."

As a student at U.C. Berkeley, Spector secretly shot thousands of feet of film in the Ladies Room of a gas station and edited it into a half-hour parade of women marching in and out of one stall. He called it "Flushed with Success." It ran at a Greenwich Village movie theater for two years, becoming an acclaimed addition to the bill of fare. Regular customers of the theater saw the movie so many times that they gave names to each of the women and would call out, "Relief is just a minute away, Sally," or, "Rhoda, sit down and relax!"

Throughout his career, Spector continued to play his games in bizarre low-budget movies that made just enough money to finance his next opus. This endeared him to some intellectuals and fringe critics, though not to mainstream audiences.

In high school, George Richmond wasn't yet an intellectual, but he became a fan of Nelson Spector's films because Cassie Carlson starred in them.

"He knew how to milk the media," Julie said. "*Maman's* first film, 'Caprice', was supposedly based on an avant-garde novel that didn't have much of a plot."

"It didn't have much of *anything,*" George said. "I guess you had to be stoned to understand it."

"Spector had a big press conference where he showed off the author, a happy pot-head who made a couple of unintelligible comments and refused to answer any questions."

"Which was a good hook for publicity."

"Then Spector wrote a screenplay that discarded everything but the title of the book," Julie said.

"And he followed up with his *international* search for a leading lady," George added.

"When he found *Maman*, he said she was the 'perfect package: beauty plus talent. And the camera loves her.'"

"She *was* beautiful," George said.

Throbbing with teenage passion, he wrote an essay about her for his English class: "Her sensitive azure eyes are as blue as a clear summer sky. She smiles a warm, dreamy smile that melts your bones. And she has a voice like velvet music."

His English teacher wasn't impressed: "But she can't act!"

Even then, George had to admit that she didn't have much talent. Not that it mattered to him.

"'Caprice' laid a well-deserved egg," Julie said. "And *Maman's* performance was trashed. Also well-deserved."

"It *was* an awful movie," George agreed, "but I saw it three times in four days. And each time, I applauded when it was over. No one else did."

Julie studied George's face for a moment.

"I suppose you want to meet her?"

"That would be great. Don't worry. I'll sit in the back of the lecture hall. It's a late afternoon class. Maybe afterwards..."

"Afterwards...?"

"...I could take you both out to dinner."

"Well..."

"Please," George said, with the look of a love-smitten teenager.

Julie laughed.

"We'd be delighted," she said.

George's wife Helen, a successful interior designer, was a practical woman. Even as a teenager, she had wasted no time on romantic daydreams. She was too busy planning her career.

When George told her he was going to meet Cassie Carlson, she asked, "What's a Cassie Carlson?"

"You don't remember her?"

"Should I?" Helen wondered.

He explained who Cassie was and why he wanted to meet her.

Helen nodded. "She was a skinny little blond, right?"

George winced.

"Slim," he said.

"She's an old lady now," Helen said. "Wrinkles. False teeth. Not a pretty sight, I'm sure."

George ignored her prediction.

"Anyway, I won't be home for dinner on Wednesday."

Helen smiled and said, "If you decide to run away with her, don't run too fast. She might have a heart attack."

True to his word, George sat in the last row of the lecture hall. From that distance, Cassie Carlson resembled the Oklahoma coed of his teenage dreams.

She still had a "slim" figure and her gray hair echoed the blonde shade of her youth. Her smile still glowed. And her voice was still strong and sweet.

Julie told the class the story of her mother's career and then showed brief clips from each of Cassie's movies. It was a truly merciful selection: she managed to find the rare flecks of gold in the dross of Cassie's oeuvre.

The rest of the period was devoted to questions and answers.

Q. "Did you always dream of being a movie star?"

A. "No, dear. That was quite a surprise."

Q. "Did you have much acting experience."

A. "I was in the drama club for three years, but I was never one of the stars."

Q. "Why do you think Nelson Spector picked *you* out of all the thousands of girls he auditioned?"

A. "He told me he listened to his heart, and his heart told him I was the one." (Smiling) "In other words, he had no idea why."

George was pleased. Cassie was gracious and unpretentious. And today he would finally meet her.

George waited until the last student had left the lecture hall before he approached Julie and Cassie.

Up close, he could almost trace the outlines of Cassie's young face beneath her wrinkled skin, like an artist's sketch beneath the surface of a painting.

And her eyes are still as blue as a clear summer sky.

"Maman, this is a colleague of mine, George Richmond," Julie said. "He's a big fan of yours."

Cassie laughed. "There aren't many of *those*. Hello, George."

She extended her hand and George shook it. Her grip was decisive.

"It's a great pleasure to meet you, Ms. Bergerac," George said.

"Cassie, please."

"Cassie."

"Juliette tells me that you're taking us out to dinner."

"Yes," George said. "She thought you might like a place called the Golden Slipper. It's only a few blocks away. Very eclectic, with a hint of French cuisine."

"A hint would be more than enough," Cassie said. "I've eaten quite a lot of French food in my time. I might be in the mood for a cheeseburger!"

In fact, Cassie didn't order a cheeseburger at the Golden Slipper. She selected *moules marinière* with *frites* and picked an expensive (and delicious) white wine to accompany it.

Although *moules* didn't appeal to him, George echoed her order. Julie chose a *Salade Niçoise.*

"George has DVD's of all your films," Julie said, as they sampled the wine.

"I still enjoy them," George said.

Cassie's blue eyes widened. "Do you?"

George blushed. "Well, I enjoy *you* in them."

Cassie thought for a moment.

"I made seven movies," she said. "Three in English, with Spector. And four in French, with Henri. In the last one, it was just a cameo."

"I have them all."

"I was better in French," Cassie said. "My accent was pretty good."

"It was," George agreed.

"But at the time I had taken only two years of college French."

"How did you...?"

"I learned some of my lines phonetically," Cassie said. "Half the time, I didn't know what the hell I was saying."

"*Maman* speaks French like a native now," Julie remarked.

"I hope so. I'm almost a native, although a Frenchman would never agree," Cassie said. "But I've lived in France for most of my life."

"You didn't come home often?" George asked.

"To see my folks, yes. But they passed away years and years ago. My home was with Henri and Juliette, and they were in France."

"You grew up there, Julie?"

"Yes," she said. "I studied film-making there at *La Fémis* in Paris. It's a school the government set up in the eighties."

"If you're French," Cassie added, "it costs you about five hundred dollars. If you're not French, about fifteen thousand."

"I guess it pays to be French," George said.

"I did my graduate work at NYU," Julie said. "And stayed to teach."

"But you'll always have Paris," George said, imitating Humphrey Bogart's "Casablanca" voice.

Cassie and Julie laughed politely.

"We also spent a lot of time in a big farm house near Aix-en-Provence," Cassie said. "Our country hideaway."

"Bob and I and the kids have spent a lot of summers there," Julie said. "And at *Maman's* apartment in Paris, too."

"And despite all the terrible things that have happened lately," Cassie added, "Paris is still Paris."

"And you never wanted to get back into films?" George asked.

"Never," Cassie said "When Henri was directing me, he had to lead me by the hand. He interpreted everything, told me how to act, how to *re*act."

"It worked."

Cassie nodded. "Henri called me *ma belle parrot*—my pretty parrot."

"I think your best film was 'En Pleine Air'," George said.

Cassie smiled.

"Those love scenes with Alain Delon!" she said. "Not a bad way to make a living."

"I think *Papa* got a little jealous," Julie said.

"Maybe a *little*."

"The scene at the dock," George said. "Very powerful."

"I suppose so. But to be honest, George, I shouldn't have been in any of those movies."

"I don't agree," George said. "There was something special about you."

Cassie's blue eyes looked off into the distance.

"Until I opened my mouth. I wasn't an actress. I would have been better off if I had stayed in Tulsa and married Steve Swanson," Cassie said.

She put her hand gently on Julie's arm and added, "But of course, then I wouldn't have my wonderful daughter."

"It's okay, *Maman*. I understand."

"I know you do, dear. What I mean is, the whole movie-star thing was a mistake. I got swept up in it, but it was a mistake."

The entrees arrived. George ate one or two mussels and a few fries. Cassie and Julie enjoyed their food enthusiastically.

After a polite pause, George said, "Julie told me you weren't too fond of Nelson Spector."

Cassie nodded. "There was nothing real about him. He was empty. Nasty. Didn't care about anyone."

"He had a vogue for a while," Julie said.

"His next 'discovery', the one after me, shot him." Cassie laughed heartily. "She said he cut her best scene out of the movie."

Julie snickered. "Didn't kill him, unfortunately."

"Henri was different," Cassie said. "He was a sweet man. Very kind. And very talented."

"He made some great films," George said.

"Not the ones I was in," Cassie said. "And we finally agreed that I should stop trying to be something I wasn't. That was the best decision we ever made."

"No," Julie disagreed. "Your best decision was having me."

Cassie smiled. "Of course it was."

"And you never missed working in the movies?" George asked.

"I was a college kid from Oklahoma who was suddenly supposed to be someone else. Someone glamorous. And talented. I was supposed to be Cinderella, I guess. But the glass slipper didn't fit."

George watched Cassie Carlson Bergerac eat her *moules* and *frites* and drink her wine. He could still see the faint outlines of her young face beneath her aging skin. She still had her sweet, bone-melting smile. And her clear blue eyes.

But after all, as George knew, what Cassie had been forty years ago had never really mattered. To him, as to all romantic young men, what mattered was what she *seemed* to be.

Strangers

The stranger has no friend, unless it be a stranger.
—Gulistan, Sa'di

Jonah Morse didn't approve of working late.

"I don't waste time at the office," he would say. "One fifteen-minute coffee break in the morning. A half-hour lunch at my desk. A well-planned work day. No need for overtime."

But that night in October, Jonah had no choice. His boss, Donald Mercer, wanted the marketing plan for the Rise&Shine Clock Radio a week ahead of time.

"On my desk at eight tomorrow morning," Mercer said. "Pressure from the sixth floor."

That was where the company's top management roosted.

So Jonah finished the plan, printed eight copies, kept one and put the rest on Mercer's desk.

It was after eleven when he left the office.

He picked up his car in the building's underground garage and drove toward the West Side Highway.

Jonah lived in Dobbs Ferry, a suburban town north of New York City. His wife, Emma, had inherited the house from her mother.

"We couldn't afford to buy it," he said. "We were lucky."

It was a windy, rainy night.

When he called Emma to say he'd be late, she warned him to be careful driving home.

"Take your time," she said. "Don't rush."

There wasn't another car in sight. As Jonah neared the West Side Highway, a man suddenly dashed out from between two parked cars, a blurred shadow in the dim yellow mist of the headlights. Jonah couldn't stop in time. He hit the man.

Automatically, hardly knowing what he was doing, Jonah turned off the engine, switched on his emergency lights and got out of the car. The man was curled up on his belly in a strange, twisted pose. Adrenaline kicking in, Jonah rushed to his side.

The man wore shabby clothes, derelict's clothes. Jonah knew he should check to see if he was still alive, but he didn't want to touch him.

The rain pelted both of them with sheets of icy water. Jonah crouched over the body, looking for signs of life but the man didn't move or make a sound.

Jonah took his cell phone from his jacket pocket and dialed 911.

"I've just had an accident," he reported calmly. "A man ran out in front of my car. I think he's dead."

He gave the operator his name and location.

"We'll send a patrol car and an ambulance," the operator said. "Stay where you are."

Jonah wanted to shield himself from the rain but he didn't get back into his car. When he looked past the spot where the man had appeared, he saw a deep-set freight entrance.

That's probably where he was sleeping, Jonah thought.

He decided to wait there until the police arrived.

It was dark in the freight entrance. Jonah turned on the cell phone light.

There was a crude cardboard shelter braced against one wall.

The loading dock probably isn't being used any more. He was living here.

Jonah approached the shelter. He hesitated for a moment, then crouched down and entered. He was struck by a cloud of foul odors. There was a makeshift mattress of rags piled up in one corner, a blanket, a couple of unopened cans of sardines, some magazines, an empty wine bottle. And a digest-size leather-jacketed book.

Jonah picked up the book. He focused the cell phone light on the cover. It was a diary.

He didn't open the book. He put it in his coat pocket.

I should give it to the police, he thought.

But he knew he wouldn't.

Jonah stood at the edge of the freight entrance, waiting for the police.

He was cold and wet. A few cars passed his, skirting around it.

I wonder if they saw the body, he thought. *Would I stop if I saw it?*

He watched the rain bounce off the roof of his car. He couldn't see the body lying in the gutter, but the image of it was frozen in his memory.

He had killed someone. It wasn't his fault. The man had run out in the middle of the block. No one could have reacted quickly enough.

The man was homeless. A derelict.

For Jonah, morality was rarely about good versus evil. It was about order and stability versus chaos. He took comfort in living by the rules. Not cheating on his income tax. Not cheating on his wife.

But this accident had opened the door to chaos.

Anyone could have killed that man. It just happened to be me.

Jonah was a killer because Don Mercer wanted his marketing plan a week ahead of schedule.

That's ridiculous. Unfair.

Why had he taken the derelict's diary? Why was he keeping it a secret?

Because I have to know who he is, Jonah decided. *Who he was.*

He heard the approaching sirens of the patrol car and the ambulance, a chorus of banshees. Jonah glanced at his watch. It was almost midnight. It had stopped raining.

He went back out into the street.

The flashing lights of the patrol car turned the scene into a lurid nightmare. The EMTs—a stone-faced young woman and a weary middle-aged man—confirmed that the victim was dead.

"Probably died instantly," she said, without a trace of sympathy.

A husky Latino policeman (his partner stayed in the patrol car) examined the body and found no wallet or ID. He took Jonah's name and address, checked his driver's license and asked him to describe the accident.

"He ran out *there*," Jonah said. "I couldn't stop in time."

The policeman nodded.

"Before you came, I went into that alley to get out of the rain. He may have been living there."

The policeman followed Jonah into the freight entrance.

"Over there," Jonah said.

The policeman switched on his flashlight and examined the cardboard shelter. He disappeared inside it for a few minutes.

When he came out, he said, "Nothing to identify him. He's a lost soul."

They returned to the scene of the accident.

"I've got all the information I need, Mr. Morse," the policeman said, with a friendly smile. "That's it, as far as you're concerned. We'll take over from here."

"It's a shame," Jonah said.

"Are you okay?"

"Yes. A little shaky, but I'm fine."

"You need someone to take you home?"

"No, I don't. Thanks."

The policeman pointed to the front of Jonah's car and said, "You have some minor damage here on the right side but your headlights are still working. Doesn't look serious."

I killed a man and my car hardly noticed it.

"If I was you," the policeman said, "I'd tell your insurance company you hit a deer."

He laughed and added, "Tell them you didn't kill it, but you knocked the hell out of it!"

That's what Jonah told his insurance company. And that's what he told his wife.

According to Don Mercer, "The sixth floor loved your marketing plan. Good work."

Jonah knew Mercer had taken credit for the plan. That was one of the rules of the corporate game. But at bonus time, Mercer always rewarded him.

As Jonah told Emma, "I wouldn't want his job, working with all those big egos on the sixth floor. I'm better off where I am."

For a week after the accident, Jonah tried not to think about what had happened on that rainy night. He put the dead man's unopened diary in a desk drawer in his home office. But the image of the crumpled, twisted body hovered in his mind's eye, a phantom that haunted his memory.

For a couple of weeks, he drove to work in a rented car and followed his well-planned work schedule.

One night, he dreamed he was on trial as a scofflaw. He was on the witness stand and the prosecutor, who looked like Don Mercer, was holding an armful of traffic tickets and kept repeating, "Guilty as charged!"

That was all he could remember of the dream.

On Thursday evening, he and Emma made their customary call to their son Edgar, a sophomore at Ithaca College. Edgar was his usual unresponsive self.

After the call, Jonah said, "He never tells us anything that matters."

"It's just a stage he's going through," she lied. "It'll pass."

Do we really know him? Even as a child, he always seemed to be in hiding.

They had delayed starting a family for more than ten years after they were married. Emma was teaching history at Vassar and working on her Ph.D. thesis. She didn't want to take time out. Later, she was still in no hurry to have a baby.

Jonah was reluctant to become a parent. His father, long dead, was a remote, passive man, not much of a role model.

But Jonah and Emma had a child because married couples were supposed to have children.

Emma was thirty-seven when she gave birth to Edgar. Her pregnancy was painful and debilitating. She spent the final month on total bed rest. And after hours of futile labor, she had a Caesarian section.

Although she told Jonah she wouldn't go through that again, she didn't blame Edgar. She and Jonah tried to love him. But childless for so long, they had developed a comfortable structure to their lives. From the beginning, their son brought disorder to that orderly world. An unwelcome intrusion.

And Edgar knew it.

When Edgar went away to college, Emma began to sleep late on Sundays. Jonah didn't need the alarm clock to wake him. He was always up at six-thirty or seven at the latest. At eleven-thirty, he would bring Emma breakfast in bed and the New York Times Book Review. (They subscribed to the Sunday Times.)

"It makes me feel like a queen," she told their friends.

On those mornings, he enjoyed a different kind of luxury: his own private time.

Early on a Sunday morning almost three weeks after the accident, Jonah was at the desk in his home office, drinking coffee and eating a toasted, buttered blueberry muffin. He took the diary out of the drawer.

The leather cover was stained. The word "Diary," elegantly embossed on it, was barely visible. The brass clasp was broken.

Too late for secrets anyway, Jonah thought.

He opened the book. The pages were unlined, tinted pale blue. Several of them had been carelessly torn out, leaving jagged remnants behind.

Jonah leafed through the book. There were only a few entries, brief chunks of text separated by empty spaces or blank pages. The handwriting was inconsistent—sometimes clear and precise, sometimes stressed and erratic, crawling up and down the page.

He read the first section. It began...

This was a woman's diary. For only a couple of weeks. She threw it away. Don't know why. Don't care.

Can't write a diary. Too many days I don't remember. black holes. Time's a blur.

Not writing for anyone else. Memories. That's all we are. I want to hold onto my memories.

I'm Peter Conrad. 61 years old.

Earliest memories. Parents. Handsome. Intelligent.

Mother plays violin. Bursts of melody. Pillars of sound. Child prodigy.

Heifitz praised her.

Never praised anyone else, she said.

Quit at top of her game. Bored, she said. 35 years old.

Father. Chemist. MIT. Started cosmetics company.

Silly business, he said. Made a fortune. Quit in his forties.

We traveled everywhere. lived everywhere. Paris, Hong Kong, Majorca, everywhere. Never stayed long enough to make friends.

Never needed anyone else.

(hardly ever.)

They loved each other. But they made love to others.

So many ways to love, Mother said.

So many beautiful women, Father said. So many handsome men.

They taught me well. Taught me well.

The first section ended there.

Now the crumpled body had a name. The beginnings of a history.

Peter Conrad. Sixty-one years old.

Wealthy, successful parents. Living in beautiful places.

A derelict now. What happened?

Jonah tried to imagine Peter Conrad's childhood.

Never settling in or settling down.

Peter's parents supposedly loved each other, but were always finding pleasure elsewhere.

That's what they taught him.

That's not what Jonah's parents taught him.

They never argued, but they weren't openly affectionate.

"We know we made the right choice when we chose each other," Mom would say, smiling at her husband. "We're content."

Dad would nod, silently smiling back at her.

When Jonah was a teenager, he asked Mom if being "content" meant being "happy."

"It's better than 'happy'," she said. "More comfortable."

She was a teacher in elementary school. At home, too, she seemed to be following a lesson plan: every event had a meaning, every story had a moral. But the Protestant God was as remote as Jonah's father. The family rarely went to church except for weddings and funerals, and on Christmas and Easter.

Morality wasn't a ladder to Heaven. It was a fortress, a safe haven from a confused and confusing world.

That's what she taught me.

His father taught him a different lesson.

On a summer Friday night when Jonah was seventeen, he took the New Haven Line to Manhattan with his friend Eddie Davidson to see "Superman" at a first-run theater on Broadway.

He and Eddie talked about women all the time and felt the customary hunger pangs for them, but neither of them had ever asked a girl for a date. Eddie was very tall, thin and shy. Jonah was a dermatologist's dream-teenager, afflicted with a case of acne that was treatable but tenacious. His less sensitive classmates called him "Zit-man."

His mother, of course, interpreted his condition as a blessing: "You'll be more mature when you start dating."

Jonah did not feel blessed.

After the movie, he and Eddie ate hot dogs and drank sodas at Orange Julius on Broadway and then started to walk crosstown to Grand Central Station. On East Forty-eighth Street Jonah saw a middle-aged man and a young woman leaving a restaurant far down the block. The man waved at an approaching taxi.

Jonah put his arm out to stop Eddie and said, "Wait a minute."

"What's the matter?"

"Just wait a minute."

The man was his father, who was supposed to be working late, as he often did. Jonah didn't know who the woman was.

"What's up?" Eddie asked.

His father held the woman's hand and kissed her before they got into the cab.

"Nice, huh?" Jonah said, pointing at a pretty girl across the street.

"Yeah, very nice," Eddie agreed, with a sad smile. "Worth stopping for."

The cab pulled away from the curb.

Jonah had just learned a lesson from his father: being content wasn't the same as being happy.

Jonah didn't wait until the next Sunday morning to read more of Peter Conrad's diary.

At dinner on Wednesday he told Emma he had brought home some work to do that evening.

"They're always taking advantage of you," she complained.

"I guess I'm indispensable."

"Then they should pay you more."

"End-of-year appraisals are coming soon," Jonah said. "Mercer needs me. I'm sure I'll do well."

Jonah's office at the back of the house was a cozy room, big enough for a desk, chair and bookcase. A heavy pocket door served as a barrier between the office and the outside world. A narrow window over the desk looked out at the back yard where a steel swing set was a forlorn reminder of Edgar's childhood.

The next section of the diary...

My sister Amelia. three years older. More enchanting than Mother.

Amelia danced. Tall, slender. Long dark hair swirling.

Amelia danced and danced.

on a beach somewhere, very young, she danced on the edge of the ocean, danced on the beach. Where was the beach? Don't remember.

I watched her. So lovely.

Sweet. sweet kisses.

She held me. I could feel her heart beating.

My heart beat faster.

My first love.

But always a sad smile.

Her time was running out. She knew it.

I have to hurry, she said.

Dead at 18.

Still see her dancing on the beach. in the water.

Still feel her heartbeat.

Missed her. Mourned her.

My parents didn't mourn. Wouldn't mourn.

Father said, People you love. Happiness. Life. You lose them all. No time to mourn.

I took the time.

Jonah had an older sister, too. Rachel.

She didn't die. If she *had* died, he would have mourned her, because that was the right thing to do. But he wouldn't have missed her. He lived in her shadow and he couldn't understand why.

Rachel acted as if her time was running out. It wasn't.

She danced, too. With the wrong men.

When she was seventeen, Rachel danced with her thirty-year-old married high school math teacher.

Jonah's father wasn't worried.

"She's nobody's fool," he said.

Jonah's mother warned Rachel to be careful.

When she got pregnant, both of them were disappointed, but neither of them seemed surprised or angry.

"Why do you always forgive her?" Jonah asked his mother. "No matter what she does? If I did half the things she does..."

"But you wouldn't," his mother said. "I trust you to do the right thing."

"If I didn't, would you forgive me, too?"

"Of course I would," his mother said.

He didn't believe her.

"Rachel needs us more," his mother said.

He didn't believe that either.

Rachel had an abortion, paid for by her father.

Afterward, she continued to break the rules. His mother continued to forgive her. And Jonah continued to do the right thing.

There was a drawing at the top of the next page of Peter Conrad's diary. A sketch of a woman's face, a fascinating face. Only a few lines, but remarkably complete, remarkably alive.

Another entry began on that page...

Marisa. Spring afternoon. Luxembourg gardens.

The bandstand. *a capella* chorus singing.

Seeing her was seeing Amelia again.

So much forgotten but not you, Marisa, dancing with the music.

Left the park with you.

Marisa. not your name.

"I like it better than mine."

I never knew your real name.

Making love night after night. young bodies. So much to give. So much to feel.

Magical.

My first love? My second love?

One day you said you had to leave me.

Can't be chained, you said. Need to wander. Need a new name.

I wanted to go with you. I'll change my name, I said.

You said no.

The time with you. Magical.

Never again that magic.

Jonah's first love was Sarah. They were both in their middle twenties, entry-level in the Marketing Department.

Sarah was just under six feet tall, almost as tall as Jonah. She moved gracefully, athletically. Her face was sharply contoured. Her gray eyes were spirited, proud.

Jonah couldn't stop watching her, thinking about her, but it wasn't easy for him to ask her out. He was afraid that she would turn him down.

She didn't.

"I'm surprised you asked," she said. "You seem a little shy."

Jonah blushed.

"Shy..." he repeated, his voice trailing off.

"I'm sorry. I didn't mean that as an insult."

"Well, it's not exactly a compliment," Jonah teased.

"You're right. Sorry. I guess that was a little insensitive. Will you forgive me?"

"I'll try," he grinned.

Their first date—dinner and a movie—started a little awkwardly for him. But Sarah was so free and comfortable with herself that her spirit seemed to wrap itself around Jonah. To unlock him.

When he kissed her goodnight he pressed his body against hers, caressed the long, firm muscles of her back and thighs, felt the soft mounds of her breasts against his chest. He couldn't believe how much he wanted her.

Three dates later, they made love in her apartment. She was so strong, alive, fiercely passionate, that it frightened Jonah. It opened a door he had never opened before. He tried to match her passion. He couldn't. And he began to wonder if he *should*. He wasn't afraid of sin, but of the chaos churning inside him.

Late one night, as Sarah lay in his arms, she said, "Let's run away."

Still feeling the pleasure of their lovemaking, it wasn't easy to focus on what she was saying.

He could only ask, "Why? Where?"

She turned in his arms, her fierce gray eyes searching his face.

"Europe maybe. South America. An adventure. Somewhere. Anywhere. You and I."

"What about our jobs?"

"The hell with them."

"Money?"

"We have enough."

"Do we?"

She kissed him. Bit his lower lip.

"We'll take a chance," she whispered.

"I don't know if I can," Jonah said.

She sat up in bed, looked down at him. The moonlight streaming through the window set fire to her eyes.

"I can't be one thing all my life," she said. "I have to be many things. Many people. I have to live a thousand different lives."

"A thousand different lives," he repeated.

"Come with me, Jonah," Sarah said. "You can. You have it in you."

He knew this was a moment that mattered. This was a choice that mattered.

"I can't," Jonah said.

She could. She left her job. To live a thousand different lives.

He couldn't.

He met Emma a few months later.

He married Emma.

Never again that magic.

Jonah finished reading Peter Conrad's diary early on a chilly, rainy Sunday morning, a morning that reminded Jonah of *that night*.

He knew that the final reading wouldn't take long. There were only three brief entries remaining, followed by a sheaf of empty blue pages.

He sat at his desk holding the diary in his hands, but not opening it. He watched the leafless trees sway in the wind, reaching for the sky with their skeletal branches. Soft, watery bullets of rain splattered against the window.

This morning it will be over, he thought.

He didn't want it to be over. He didn't want to stop sharing those fragments of another man's life, a taste of another *kind* of life.

At last, he couldn't delay any longer.

The first passage was written in an almost indecipherable scrawl...

Lenore. San Francisco. walking uphill running downhill!

Long nights overnight at Barney's Place jazz absinthe

Beach at Carmel. Folk songs Marie black hair black eyes. spanish love songs

Sweet lips breasts thighs passion

time's a blur Night to day to night to day

Can't find the memories

Can't

The second passage...

while I slept someone stole my wallet. ID cards. Money $3. Photos of Amelia Mother Father Marisa. Everything that was me. Now it will be easier to do.

The last passage...

For days now my mind is clear. My memory is clear. Too clear.

Amy my wife my loving beloved wife said not to drive home. Stay here tonight, she said. Amanda my loving beloved daughter just 17 said not to drive home. I'm fine I said. Only had a couple of drinks. A few puffs of pot.

They were right. I was wrong.

They died. I didn't.

No reason to stay here. To stay anywhere.

The next page was blank.

There'll be nothing to read next Sunday morning, Jonah thought.

Peter Conrad had died, taking most of his memories with him.

Jonah sat watching the rain for a few minutes. He absently drank the cold coffee remaining in his cup and ate the last piece of blueberry muffin.

The trees were still trying in vain to touch the clouds with their bony fingers. The storm was still firing its soft bullets at the window.

Suddenly, Jonah smiled. He picked up a pen that was lying on the desk. He looked down at the blank diary page for several minutes. Then he began to write...

No sense letting go of life.

Went back to Paris. To places I remember.

Great wine. Great food. Great women.

Searching for Marisa. Wonder what her name is now.

I'll find her. I know I will.

Jonah smiled again and closed the diary.

It was a small beginning. But it *was* a beginning.

Sunday after Sunday, month after month, Jonah continued his adventures—or were they Peter Conrad's adventures? After a while, it didn't seem to matter.

The world of the diary never touched the everyday world he lived in, never changed that world. It was his secret refuge.

Wherever he "traveled", he felt at home. He never found Marisa. But in Rio de Janeiro, by chance, he met Sarah. She said she was proud of him now. They shared a passionate month but they didn't stay together. They each had other lives to live.

When Jonah had filled every page, he would go back now and then to remember, to read again what Peter had written and what he himself had written.

And there came a time when he began to believe that he had written it all.

Joanna Yesterday

I met Joanna yesterday. After being apart for thousands of yesterdays.

We were in San Francisco. Touristy Union Square.

"Is that you, Jesse?" she wondered.

She recognized me despite the extra pounds around my middle, my thinning hair.

"Joanna?"

She looked almost the same. Still in a hurry. A focused look, a purposeful stride. Her dark hair (now touched with gray), cut shorter but still out of control. And that crooked half-smile, as if every funny story had a sad ending.

We hesitated. Should we shake hands? Kiss? Shake *and* kiss?

We shook hands and kissed awkwardly, a fleeting gesture to the past.

* * *

In Manhattan's Central Park, many yesterdays ago, we sat on a bench by the Pond, held hands, kissed.

"I wish today could be forever," Joanna said.

"Why can't it be?"

"Today always becomes yesterday."

We had met at a party a few weeks earlier in an apartment on the Upper West Side. A terrible party. I can't remember why we were there or who invited us. It was noisy, crowded. Boring people. We found each other.

"We don't belong here," she said.

"Let's have a drink somewhere else," I said.

"Who are you?"

"Jesse."

"Joanna."

We found a place a few blocks away. The Poet's Corner. That's why she chose it.

"I write poetry," she said.

"I can barely *read* it," I said and she laughed.

We shared a bottle of the least expensive red wine.

Joanna recited one of her poems. About following a trail of footprints in the snow. But a fresh snowfall covers the trail and it disappears.

I almost remember the last line. “And the gates to that mystery closed forever.” Something like that, but better.

I told her I didn’t understand her poem but it was definitely poetic.

She smiled and took my hand in hers.

I looked down at her hand. On her left index finger was a slim silver band, a snake swallowing its own tail.

“The Worm Ouroboros,” she said.

“If you say so.”

“No beginning, no end. Yesterday, today and tomorrow flow into each other, repeating themselves over and over.”

“Not for me,” I said. “Today is different from all my yesterdays. I met you.”

“Very poetic,” she said, approvingly.

I lifted her hand and kissed the ring.

“That’s for today,” I said. “And tomorrow.”

We began to see each other most nights, most days. She had graduated from Columbia two years ago.

I was working in a corporate TV studio. I had graduated from NYU three years ago.

After a month or so, she moved into my apartment.

* * *

Joanna and I found a San Francisco place to have a drink, off the tourists’ route.

“Sorry it’s not The Poet’s Corner,” I said.

“Don’t be. I’m not a poet anymore.”

“Why not?”

She smiled her half-smile.

“Not enough talent,” she said.

“I’m sorry.”

“I’m not. Can’t fool yourself forever.”

“Still teaching?”

“Yes.”

“Still enjoying it?”

Joanna shook her head. “Routine. Same old, same old.”

✵ ✵ ✵

Joanna opened the envelope, read the letter, smiled and said, "Columbia University Press. They're publishing my poems!"

I embraced her. Kissed her.

"We'll celebrate tonight," I said.

She was crying.

"A new beginning," I said.

That night we had an expensive dinner, drank expensive wine and were too drunk to make love. The next morning, we remedied that.

Joanna's poetry was ignored by reviewers. Except the critic for one small, snobbish literary magazine.

"Her work is pedestrian and derivative. This is an inauspicious debut."

I comforted her in my prosaic fashion. She didn't take comfort.

Finally Joanna said, "I won't give up. I'll work harder."

She did. And she was ready to take on the world again.

In six months, she had completed a new collection of poems. Columbia University Press rejected it. So did every other publisher.

Joanna wasn't discouraged. She self-published her book. Distributed it to reviewers, her colleagues in Academia. Publicized it with news releases, readings in a few book stores.

No one cared.

This time, Joanna didn't bounce back. She pulled in her petals, a flower starving for light. I tried to be the sun but I didn't shine brightly enough.

When my boss at the corporate TV studio was promoted, I got his job. I liked being the boss.

Joanna tried to share in my success. She couldn't.

We had been together for almost two years. She left me.

✵ ✵ ✵

"What brings you to San Francisco?" I asked.

"MLA Convention," Joanna said.

"MLA?"

"Modern Language Association."

"Should I know what that is?"

"Academics," Joanna said, as if that were an insult. "I'm reading a paper."

"About poetry."

"Wallace Stevens. The usual shit."

“You don’t seem very happy about it,” I said.

“I’m looking for a new job,” she confessed. “That’s why I’m here. The MLA Convention is the scholar’s meat market. I’m on display.”

“Where are you teaching now?” I asked.

“Marymount in Manhattan. I need a change. Something on the West Coast, I hope.”

I looked down at her hands.

“You’re married,” I said.

“Divorced,” Joanna said. “Three years ago. The ring keeps most men away.”

“Do you have any children?”

“A daughter. Eleven years old. She’s staying with my mother while I’m here.”

“Is she a poet?”

“Not if I can help it,” Joanna said.

“Is she looking forward to the West Coast?”

“She’s mad at me. Doesn’t want to leave her friends.”

A daughter, I thought.

* * *

A weekend blizzard in Manhattan when we were still living together. Not a disaster. By Monday morning, the streets would be drivable, walkable.

A weekend blizzard with Joanna. Lazy, sexy, food and wine. Turner Classic Movies. Jazz albums. A cozy oasis in the snow.

“You don’t feel guilty?” I asked. “About not writing, I mean.”

This was before she had finished her first book of poetry. Before Columbia University Press had accepted it. Before she had begun to feel the chill of reality.

We were eating home-cooked spaghetti marinara. Drinking Chianti. Listening to a Coltrane album “for Lovers.”

“I’ve been writing my ass off,” Joanna said. “I *deserve* a break.”

“I hope you have some ass left. I love your ass. I *deserve* your ass.”

She leaned across the table and kissed me with tomato-sauced lips.

“Delicious,” I said.

After some additional kisses, we returned to our food.

“How many kids do you plan to have?” I wondered.

Joanna frowned. “Kids?”

“Don’t you ever think about that?”

"No."

"Think about it," I suggested.

"I don't even know if I'll ever get married. Let alone *kids*."

Silence for a minute or two.

"Do *you* want kids?" Joanna asked.

"Yes."

"Why?"

"That's what people do. They have kids."

"Jesus Christ, Jesse! People also commit murder. Doesn't mean *you* have to!"

I smiled and said, "That's what is called a false equivalence."

Joanna shook her head.

"I have my work to do," she said. "Poetry to write. That's what people like *me* do. Marriage? Children? I don't think so."

"Well. Let's suppose you become a Nobel-prize-winning poet. The Poet Laureate of the World."

"Sounds good to me."

"And you decide to get married and have kids. Would you want sons or daughters or doesn't it matter to you?"

Joanna thought for a moment and said, "Sons. Only sons."

"Because?"

"I don't like women. Never had a really close girlfriend."

"What don't you like about women?"

"They're either too aggressive," she said, "trying to outdo men. Or they're too *passive*-aggressive."

"All women?"

"I don't trust them. I don't want to create another one."

"Then you should have male children only."

"You've got that right," Joanna said. "Men are so much easier to deal with. They're so fucking obvious."

"I think that's an insult."

Joanna reached out and stroked my hair.

"You see, sweetheart? You can't even tell when you're being insulted."

* * *

"Why are you in San Francisco, Jesse?"

"I'm shooting a movie," I said. "For H.B.O."

"Really?"

"I'm a director. I've made several films. TV shows, too."

Joanna was surprised. But not impressed.

"I never watch TV," she said, "except PBS. I don't go to the movies much. When I do, it's an art film."

"That's not my style," I said. "You remember: I'm not a poet. I make action films. Car chases. Westerns."

"Do you enjoy that?"

"Yes. And it pays well."

Joanna looked down at my hand.

"You're married," she said.

"For fourteen years. A son ten years old, and a daughter eight."

"Are you happy?"

"Most of the time. Which is more than I ever expected."

Joanna smiled her funny-sad smile.

"My husband got tired of me," she said. "In the beginning, I was spending most of my free time writing, which he resented."

"I guess I can understand that."

"But when I gave up writing, when I needed his support, his sympathy, he didn't have any to spare."

Her voice was so soft, it was as if I were remembering her words rather than hearing them.

"I know this sounds corny," I said, "but you're still young, Joanna."

"I don't feel young," she said.

There were tears in her eyes.

Her hands were clasped on the table in front of her. On her left index finger was a slim silver band, a snake swallowing its own tail.

"The Worm Ouroboros," I said.

"Yesterday, today and tomorrow," she whispered.

But the Worm was a myth.

I could see that Joanna today was nothing like Joanna yesterday. And never would be again.

Readers Guide

Please be aware that the Readers Guide may contain spoilers.

"Prologue: Storytellers"

1.When you were growing up, did your parents and grandparents tell you stories about their youth, their struggles, their joys and your family's history? Do you think they sometimes stretched the truth? Why?

2. Have you continued that storytelling tradition? Do you ever stretch the truth?

"Why I Never Got Married"

1. What is the relationship between Angela and her uncle (the narrator)? Is he the "old grouch" he claims to be?

2. Discuss whether or not his improbable story answers her question.

"Hugo's Voice"

1. Hugo Strauss "could rarely find the right words." Why is it so difficult for him to communicate—with his wife, his best friend, his Aunt Esther and Uncle Myron—with everyone?

2. As his marriage deteriorates, Hugo vividly remembers the girl he made love to when he was sixteen. How does that memory affect his attitude toward women?

3. Hugo's mother said, "You learned the craft, but not the art." What did she mean, and how did this shape Hugo's self-image?

4. The first time he sees her, Hugo is immediately attracted to Frankie. Why does this turn out to be a major problem for him?

5. Why, after refusing to design jewelry for several years, does Hugo create a set of earrings for Frankie? What is her reaction?

6. Do you think Hugo and Frankie will fall in love? Will that love endure?

"Empathy"

1. Empathy is usually viewed in a positive light. Does empathy also have a darker side?

2. Would you want to be able to hear the "other voices" of your family and friends?

3. Would you want your family and friends to be able to hear *your* "other voice"?

"Wildwood"

1. Why is David living in the woods, far from New York City, far from what he says is the "good life"?

2. Why did the woman he was living with leave him?

3. Why does Miranda call her home Wildwood?

4. Why can't David ever find Wildwood again?

"Fair Play"

1. Is the narrator of the story playing fair with Laurel?

2. Is Laurel's mother playing fair with the narrator?

"Second Sight"

1. Would Steven Fowler and Sammy Bloomberg define a "practical man" in the same way?

2. Sammy's brother Seth was a dreamer whose dreams never came true. Did his disappointment turn him into a practical man?

3. Did Seth's disappearance change Sammy? Does it change Steven?

4. Where do you think Seth went? Another town? "A hell of a good universe next door"?

"Tiny Town"

1. Why did Mark have childhood nightmares about Tiny Town?

2. How did Mark disappoint his father? His wife? His daughter?

3. Why does Mark return to Tiny Town?

"Cassie"

1. Why is the memory of Cassie important to George Richmond?

2. How does George's wife feel about his "reunion" with Cassie?

3. Is George disillusioned by his meeting with Cassie?

"Strangers"

1. Is Jonah Morse happily married? Is he content with his career?

2. What did Jonah's mother teach him about morality? What did his father teach him?

3. Why did Jonah reject his first love, Sarah? Does he regret it?

4. What part does Peter Conrad's death, and his diary, play in Jonah's life?

"Joanna Yesterday"

1. Why did Joanna leave Jesse?

2. How has each of them changed since that time?

3. The ring that Joanna wears—the Worm Ouroboros—is a symbol of the endlessly repeating cycle of past, present and future. Why does Jesse call this symbol a myth?

www.ingramcontent.com/pod-product-compliance
Lightning Source LLC
Chambersburg PA
CBHW030613310726
48979CB00003B/688

* 9 7 8 1 6 3 2 9 3 5 6 3 2 *